THE
ONE WHO
LOVES
YOU
THE MOST

THE

ONE WHO

LOVES YOU

THE MOST

medina

LQ
LEVINE QUERIDO

MONTCLAIR | AMSTERDAM | HOBOKEN

for my mom.
in your unshakeable love, i am stronger.
in your light, you teach me how to love.

This is an Arthur A. Levine book
Published by Levine Querido

www.levinequerido.com • info@levinequerido.com
Levine Querido is distributed by Chronicle Books LLC
Copyright © 2022 by medina
Lyrics on p. v and 243 courtesy of Brett Dennen,
"The One Who Loves You The Most,"
Published by Emigrant Music and Downtown Music Publishing
Library of Congress Control Number: 2021943723
ISBN 978-1-64614-090-9
Printed and bound in China

FSC
www.fsc.org
MIX
Paper from
responsible sources
FSC® C144853

Published May 2022
First printing

When the sky is falling from above you
And the wind is raging from the coast
And you want someone who truly loves you
I will be the one who loves you the most

—Brett Dennen, "The One Who Loves You the Most"

I have never felt like I belonged to my body. Never in the way rhythm belongs to a song or waves belong to an ocean.

It seems like most people figure out where they belong by knowing where they came from. When they look in the mirror, they see their family in their eyes, in their sharp jawlines, in the texture of their hair. When they look at family photos, they see faces of people who look like them. They see faces of people who they'll look like in the future.

For me, I only have my imagination.

When I look in the mirror I imagine my birth mother looking right back at me. I study the shape of my face, the shape of my eyes, the color of my skin, and the texture of my hair. I gently push my finger along my low bridge in my nose that can never seem to keep glasses on. In me is her, and in her, I hope, is still me.

But sometimes when I look in the mirror, I feel I see more of her than me. Because the me I see doesn't feel like me. I don't feel I belong to this face or to this body.

And then there's Mom.

My mom.

The woman I call my mom and love deeply and dearly.

My mom.

If only I could one day show her how much she means to me. I think sometimes I take her for granted. Sometimes I'm not as sensitive or compassionate as I could be.

But I'm always trying.

1

As I mindlessly pulled out grass in the park, the sounds of loud cheers startled me from my thoughts, and I saw my mom calling me over, a twinkle of joy in her eyes. A few seconds later she was standing over me, blocking the sun with her silhouette.

"This drummer is great!" she said excitedly, pointing to a street drummer using plastic bins as drums.

In New York City, everyone's got a talent, so you must be heart-stopping great to get a New Yorker to pause and watch.

We scurried over and watched in awe. I peered around long, lanky legs to try to get a better view. We stayed and listened to the boy play drums for a while, and I wasn't ready to leave just yet, but after a few minutes I could see the light in my mom's eyes fading. Her back starting to slouch, her energy shifting—I knew it was time to go. I quickly gave the drummer a dollar, gave my mom a loving look, gave her a side squeeze, and our bodies walked together to the train.

When the train arrived, we slipped in between book bags and briefcases and slid into a space big enough for the both of us. I cracked open my book, carefully pressing down the pages, proud of the progress I had made on my extra credit homework. I popped in my earbuds and pressed play on YEBBA's cover of "Weak," by SWV. My mom quietly played sudoku on her phone. I peered over at her every now and then and watched her face for any changes in expression.

My mom is an interpreter for the Deaf. I grew up learning American Sign Language before I learned English. And I was fluent in her body language and facial expressions.

"You know, you don't always have to worry about me. I'm quite all right!" my mom said after a stop or two, breaking our silence.

I put my music on pause and slid my bookmark into my book. "I'm loving you."

"You're checking in on me," she said, nudging me gently as a smile opened up like the sky after a rainstorm.

"Checking in on you is loving you," I replied softly.

When we got home, our two cats, Eliza and Cagney, greeted us as if we had gone on a long cruise around the world and they hadn't seen us in months. So dramatic, and yet that's the kind of unconditional cat love I'm always here for.

"Finish all your homework for tomorrow?" my mom asked as she clambered through the cabinets, getting ready to make dinner.

Before I could reply she answered her own question. "Of course you did! Are you sure you're not a teacher in disguise?"

I smiled and stretched out my sweatshirt to my knees to stop it clinging to my body.

My body.

Was growing in places I was increasingly becoming more and more uncomfortable about.

After dinner, we turned on *Wheel of Fortune*, but before it got to the bonus round my mom abruptly got up and said she was tired. *Tired* was usually another word for *depressed*. I know they aren't the same words, but sometimes it was easier for my mom to say a word that didn't have the same gut-punch reaction.

. . . But in all honesty, it still felt the same.

The next morning, I felt the vibration of upbeat music bouncing off the walls. I was happy for that. I wasn't sure how long it would last, but I knew I had at least one song.

Each morning was pretty routine, aside from how my mom was feeling. I got ready, walked to the bus stop, and got to school early. Some mornings, my mom drove me, but I let her take the lead on that. I never wanted to push her or make her feel she needed to do one extra thing when one thing could feel like the biggest.

Today I felt the beating of my heart telling me that Mom needed her own space. Plus, she had made a sign and put it on her door: "My soul and universe is telling me I need space right now. I'm all right. Loving you, my butterfly."

◎ ◎ ◎

When I got to homeroom, Mrs. Andersen was writing out the class lesson on the board.

READING + DISCUSSION
ESSAY PROJECT

"Good morning, Gabriela. There's something different about you. Let me see. Is that a new sweatshirt?" she asked with a smile.

I set my books down and perked up, trying to get my mom off my mind. "Good eye! It's a darker shade of black: Vantablack."

"I knew it!"

"So, what's this essay business about? I mean, what kind of essay?" I said inquisitively.

"You'll have to wait until English. I think you'll like it!" She sounded impressed. I always knew when she was impressed, which almost made me feel pressure to always be impressive.

Mrs. Andersen was right about most things. She had a special superpower of knowing her students—maybe even more than they knew or understood themselves. Probably because she read our words.

Words.

Words were music to me. I loved them. Gobbled them up like Swedish Fish.

The bell rang, and my classmates trickled in slowly one by one, some in pairs, like rain droplets.

Class had already begun, but my mind was still daydreaming. Thinking of my birth mother, my mom and her depression, and feeling extremely self-conscious about the way I looked. The way I felt.

The way I awkwardly slow-danced in my body that was changing. I no longer knew the dance steps to this song.

I looked up from my vegan leather-bound journal my mom had given me as an early birthday present and watched Mrs. Andersen's mouth move and her arms sway, like she was conducting a symphony. She was a thin white woman. She wore a black turtleneck, a small, gold necklace, impossibly small, matching stud earrings, black pants, and black clogs. I always admired her simplicity.

"Did you get all that, class?" She raised her eyebrows, trying not to smile. The middle of her forehead would crinkle in a different way when she was actually annoyed.

I stopped slouching from my desk, pulling my hand out of my oversized, black Champion hoodie.

I'd been wearing hoodies since I'd noticed my chest starting to grow. Loose T-shirts weren't cutting it anymore. The fabric was too thin, and no matter how much I pulled at it, it would always go back to clinging.

I blurted out: "Yeah, write an essay about a time we were our most authentic self and a time when we weren't. Seven hundred words. Draft due next Monday."

"Yes, and to—"

"But what do you mean by authentic self? I mean, isn't it impossible to not be your authentic self if you are always yourself? You don't walk around living someone else's life . . ."

I heard snickering behind me as I jumped back in. I didn't have to look to know it was Jonathan Kazalonis and his friends. Before she could finish, I'd interrupted, which I didn't do to be rude or anything. I just couldn't stop my mouth. Or was it my brain?

The snickering behind me continued.

"That's a philosophical point of view, Gabriela, but what I mean by being our authentic self is accepting each part of what makes us, *us*!"

She'd really emphasized *us*. She meant business. The last part of the assignment would be to share it with a partner. I had already figured out what I was going to write, but sharing it? She had to stop playing with my emotions like that.

Everyone was eyeing the clock. Four minutes until the bell.

I looked around the room to see who I could possibly share my essay with. There was Maya McKenzie. But we really didn't talk anymore—and being around her made me nervous. Not like *nervous for an exam* nervous, but nervous in the way that I couldn't feel my feet and lost all ability to speak.

Mrs. Andersen added: "Now what's different about this assignment is that you'll not only write an essay, but you'll accompany it with a piece from another medium, to enhance it."

Eyes were starting to glaze over. Without flinching, Mrs. Andersen continued. "For example, write your essay and then record a podcast that *enhances* it. I know you've never had to do anything but writing in this class, but it's getting more and more important to use different various types of mediums to present our work—"

"BECAUSE PRINT IS DYING!! BECAUSE CAPITALISM!" some classmates moaned from the back of the class.

Mrs. Andersen carefully reached for her necklace and started rubbing it for good luck. Or maybe she was making a wish. "I'm simply saying that digital media is having a moment!"

Lucy turned around and squealed with Jessica as they did their infamous handshake that probably took weeks to practice—or maybe just a few dozen times watching the remake of *The Parent Trap* and changing up one thing. They weren't really known for being original. Another example: their podcast, *Facts of Life*. A show in the '80s. Anyway, almost everyone in class had been a guest on the show.

Two minutes until the bell now. Mrs. Andersen stretched her neck up as she spoke above crinkling paper, books being stacked, backpacks being zipped, the screeching of chairs being pushed out.

"Or write your personal essay with photography. I want drafts of your essay soon. Once your draft is approved by me, you'll get the go ahead to complete the second half of your project. Your final projects will be due right before winter break. I'm giving you the semester to finish. This is an opportunity to show off your creativity! Be bold, be different, be Y-O-U."

Mrs. Andersen . . . she sounded like a really ethical shampoo commercial, but she was pretty convincing. I had gone to guitar camp last summer, but I wouldn't say I was good enough to write a song or even perform. As for any other skills, my photography skills were above average, at least for Instagram standards. I didn't think that was saying much. Everyone's a photographer on Instagram.

Now I was starting to second-guess the assignment completely. It was going to be impossible to find a different way to express myself other than writing, to sum up who I was in a project.

When you're adopted, you kind of exist in between two worlds. I wasn't sure if there was a world where I was my most authentic self. What if what people saw when they looked at me, wasn't really how I felt inside or what I wanted to see when I looked at me?

2

After my first three classes, my brain was still in a fog. I honestly didn't have any friends in Science or Social Studies, so I kept to myself. Most days, I convinced myself it was better that way. Letting people in and then having them disappear hurt too much. I also couldn't stop thinking about my English project.

The lunch bell rang like a diligent rooster and interrupted me. Maybe that was a good thing. When I got to the cafeteria, I quickly spotted the table I sat at. *My* table. Everyone in our lunch room gravitates toward a place where they feel comfortable or they feel like they fit in. This was mine.

I carefully took out my lunch, examining each container, making sure everything was there. When something is missing, I know my mom isn't doing well. But today, she had packed exactly twelve grapes, twelve almonds, a banana sliced into twelve pieces, a honey stick, and a hummus veggie wrap. The almonds, banana slices, and honey were my dessert. As usual, my mom had taped a note onto the foil of my wrap. She always thought of me.

So far this year I'd been sitting alone. Sometimes I'd eat in Mrs. Andersen's room, but people had found out I was eating lunch with her and thought it was weird, so I'd stopped. I didn't really want to give them any more reasons to think I was weird. Or more weird.

I used to sit with my best friend, but she'd moved in with her dad a few months ago. Her parents had gotten divorced. Her mom had moved in with her new girlfriend, and my bestie was going to be living mostly with her dad. He lived in another school district so that meant she would be going to a different middle school. I was still convinced she wanted to live with him because he had, like, 900 channels and her mom didn't believe in TV. She said it was damaging to your health, but that didn't stop her from using Coca-Cola or Crisco as tanning oil.

I basically felt like we weren't going to be friends this year no matter what, though, since she'd started dressing differently and flirting with boys and caring about fitting in. I cared in the sense that I would do just enough to avoid being talked about. Self-preservation was real. My mind floated in and out, thinking about my mom, thinking about school, the global economy, and centuries of unrest in the Middle East . . . Yeah . . . my mind was working overtime, always.

I normally finished eating lunch before anyone else, purposefully. Lunch wasn't about eating anyway, it was about chitchatting, gossiping, and conversations I could never seem to understand how to enter.

The rest of the day, I kept my head down, did my work, and slipped by eyes that didn't really acknowledge me.

The last bell rang, and people trampled over one another to get their weekend started. I was in no rush. The sidewalks were covered in beautiful leaves like ribbons of red and gold. I could smell the freshness of the air as I stepped into nature. I closed my eyes and stood silently as the familiar scents of autumn embraced my senses.

I daydreamed I was floating on my back in the ocean. The only thing that clung to my skin was the sun. In this daydream, I stay in the water until the sun goes down. My body is always blurry, so I can never see that it is me, but I know it is me because it feels like me. I feel free.

Soon, in this out-of-this-world daydream, I am approaching land. My body becomes more in focus, but before it becomes clear, the daydream ends. It always ends.

"Hello?" I heard a menacing voice behind me ask.

I felt my face burn like a furnace. The same voice that lingered behind me in homeroom. I awkwardly and quickly puffed out my shirt. I wanted very much to stay in my daydream and believe the voice was meant for someone else. I squeezed my eyes shut so hard I felt my eyelashes prickle me.

"Hello, what are you doing? Are you gonna move?" The voice was getting louder. The voice was definitely directed at me. I opened my eyes and turned around and saw Jonathan and his two friends gawking at me.

"I . . . ," I slowly said, feeling like I was swallowing a cotton ball.

"I . . . I . . . ," Jonathan mimicked. "You're such a weirdo, you know that? You're so queer. What even are you?"

Before I could understand what was happening, Jonathan and his friends zoomed past me on their scooters and skateboards, knocking my journal out of my hands.

At that very moment, I didn't know what came over me, but I started crying. Full on crying.

In public.

I felt like I was stung by a bee as my throat started to swell. The soft fragrances of autumn that surrounded me became this dreary and dark tornado of confusion.

I didn't know *what* I was.

3

When I got home, I threw off my shoes, tossed my bag onto the couch, and ran to my bedroom.

I could hear my mom trailing behind me, calling my name. I could tell she was worried by the sound of her voice, but I didn't respond.

"Honey, do you want to talk about it?" she said from behind my door.

"No," I muffled from under my sheets and pillow.

"I understand. We don't have to talk about it." She paused. "You hungry?"

"No," I lied. I was hungry.

"You sure? I made Grandma's famous Sicilian chicken soup. I had a little taste already. I think it's the best I've made. Cagney already stole some, and Eliza even liked it. And she doesn't like anything."

I heard her laugh and the door jiggle a bit as the light from underneath the door disappeared.

When I was adopted at age two, I was afraid of cats. I had never seen a cat before. I thought they were rats. But I learned to love cats even if they looked like fluffy rats.

Eliza was very picky for an animal that relies on being fed by humans. Cagney, on the other hand, had no off switch when it came to testing out human food. Foodie Cagney with extraordinary taste.

"I told you I'm not hungry and I don't want to talk about it," I said, burying my face farther into my pillow.

"Then let's not talk or eat," my mom replied with a soothing voice. Her voice was soft and sweet like honey. Soft, gentle, unassumingly sweet.

I got out of bed and unlocked the door, so she knew the invitation was there. Then I threw myself back onto my bed and faced the window with one eye open, waiting for her next move.

I didn't want to tell her I needed a hug. I wanted her to just know.

Time didn't pass at all as she wrapped her arms around me. We lay in silence until I finally dozed off. I felt safe in her arms.

Later that evening, I woke up to Eliza on my head, my mom's feet in my face, and a tapestry of stars glowing from the skylight window.

I was hoping my mom would forget I had been so upset and she wouldn't ask. I gently slid out of bed to grab some soup.

"Where'ya goin?" she asked with a singing smile.

"Nowhere," I said, watching her smile morph into something more serious.

"Let's go nowhere together. Now how about that soup . . ."

As my mom was warming up the soup and humming to her made-up song, with a lump in my throat I finally asked: "Is *queer* a bad word?"

The expression on her face was so neutral, I wasn't sure what she was thinking. She grabbed the soup from the microwave, spun around, sat next to me and asked, "Where did you hear it, and how was the word used?"

I felt my blood rush to my head and blurted out: "I don't know, okay! I just wanted to know if it was bad!" I didn't want to make my mom upset or worried. She had enough hard days dealing with her own life. I didn't want to add to it.

"My butterfly, words are not bad or good. It is how they are used that gives them meaning. Will you please tell me how this word made it into your life?"

Somehow, I wanted my mom's reaction to be different. I wanted her to be visibly upset, or visibly sad. I wanted an emotion I could cling to and call my own, because I wasn't sure how I was supposed to feel. All I knew was that I wanted her to know how much this word stung me, but I didn't know how a word that I had never heard before could have so much meaning or power over me. How could I not know this word? Was I *that* sheltered? I felt embarrassed.

As we sat in silence, our bowls of soup no longer created cloudlike steam. Cagney perched up on the side of the table, doing his best trying to nuzzle his way to the humans-only feast. He eventually gave up and started playing with Eliza. I tried not to crack a grin because it was only a matter of time before she would flick her tail into his face and walk away.

My mom asked again where I heard the word *queer.*

"I heard it in a movie. Someone was watching Netflix during homeroom," I lied. Why did I do that? I guess I was ashamed for not knowing something. I had a very bad habit of being a bit of a know-it-all. I owned it. *Usually.*

My mom looked at me unconvinced but didn't push me to talk further about it. In a way, I kind of wish she had, because I wasn't sure if I would get the nerve to bring it up again.

The next morning, my ears tingled as they heard the sweet sound of "Silver Springs," by Fleetwood Mac. My mom had a tradition of waking up slowly to music. Alarms had no place in our home. We'd been listening to Fleetwood Mac's album *The Dance* for the last four months, but for whatever reason "Silver Springs" was our anthem.

My body gently awakened to the drums and raspy voice of Stevie Nicks, then the song switched. The floors buzzed, and I heard a familiar voice belt out:

"You've got to get up every morning with a smile in your face . . ."

Before my feet could reach the floor, my mom, who was using our Apple TV remote as a microphone, was at the foot of my bed singing along:

"Now start getting ready because you're going to be late which will make me late, and no one wants that . . ."

She smiled as she left my room singing. Three seconds later she poked her head back in and sang:

"I'm serrrrrRRr—iiii-oooouSs."

Unlike most moms, my mom didn't have embarrassing music taste. She was so into music and knew personal stories about each artist too. She'd passed her love for music down to me. My music taste dated back to the Billie Holiday days and included all genres.

To her, music was constantly giving of unconditional love. That type of love can't be taken away, even if it seems like it can be, even if there are other forces that seem to threaten its love.

I've known about my mom's depression since I was in elementary school. She'd always had it, but when my grandpa died, it reared its ugly head back at her.

Depression is like a ghost. You can't see it, but you can feel it.

Everyone who is close to you can feel it.

Each day depression greeted us, and each day we had a choice as to how we greeted it back. We had good days and bad days. Some days we learned new ways to manage it. Other days, we sat next to depression and did our best to not let it bring us down.

And today was a good day. In fact, it was an all-around good weekend.

We spent half of Saturday in line at Trader Joe's and the rest of the time repotting plants on our terrace.

"There's something about feeling the soil in your hands, this living joy that gives life to so much of what we need," my mom said as the sun danced on the crown of her head. In that moment, I could feel her peace and happiness blooming.

First thing on Sunday morning, I checked in. She was already up sewing and humming to Roberta Flack's "The First Time Ever Saw Your Face." I decided to sleep in and cuddle with my cats for as long as possible until I had to do my homework.

I felt like an average kid, with a mom who didn't need me to help her out of bed or cook for her because she was too depressed to do anything.

It was a good weekend.

When Monday rolled around, I quickly showered, got dressed, and packed my bag for school. As I placed my last notebook into my bag, I realized I hadn't touched my English homework. I figured I'd start a new draft of my essay at school and just get it over with.

When I got downstairs, I snuggled with Eliza and Cagney as if it were the last time I would see them and scarfed down the oatmeal that was waiting for me. Then, my phone buzzed.

"Any day now." It was my mom.

I looked out the window and saw her sitting in the car laughing, looking down at her phone.

I slid into the front seat, and my mom pulled out a huge CD case from the side of her seat. She kept it old school.

"Your turn to DJ," she beamed.

I had found a cover of "All My Loving" by Amy Winehouse online last summer and made a mixtape of every cover she ever sang.

"Amy."

My mom looked at me with agreement. "Amy."

As my mom drove down the small streets, by Brooklyn brownstones and children walking toward their final destinations, we sang to Amy's magical voice.

Even though I felt like I was in the moment with my mom, my brain was still pushing me to be Elsewhere. It wasn't until we were stuck in a long line of cars that I looked out my window and saw a girl wearing a glittery purple backpack with lots of colorful pins. It made me smile and get out of my head.

When we reached a red light, I caught a closer glimpse of the huge music note she had stitched onto her bag and another pin of a flag that had five horizontal stripes: two light blue, two pink, and one white in the center. I'd never seen that flag before.

"Do you know her?" my mom asked.

"Does anyone really know anybody?" I said sarcastically.

"I'm glad you think you're funny. She looks sweet. Maybe you could be friends. Looks like she loves music too."

"A lot of people love music, Mom. Besides, I know *of* her. And I think she's in fifth grade . . . She's some kind of genius or something." I didn't know why I was so resistant to making a new friend. My door definitely wasn't being knocked down with people wanting to be my friend. But I wasn't about to be friends with a 5th grader.

"Is someone being ageist?" Mom said, smirking at me.

I ignored her comment.

"Right here's good." My mom parked a block away from the school entrance, and I popped out of the car. She signed "I love you" in sign language, and I returned the love.

When I got out of the car, the girl with the purple backpack was standing right in front of me.

4

I wasn't normally confronted with a situation like this. You know, when one second your mom was telling you that you should make friends with someone and the next second that person was standing right in front of you. Was this a sign? My mom believed in signs. Mostly, she believed anything Stevie Nicks said and that everything was put in your life for a reason.

For some reason I felt nervous. I set down my journal and bent over to tie my shoelace as a way to avoid eye contact with my potential new friend. And buy some time so I could think of the right first thing to say. Not really a great start. Not to mention my shoelace wasn't even untied, so I had to pretend to be fixing it.

As I was tying my fake-untied shoe, I heard a voice above me say: "I like your journal."

No one willingly gave me compliments, so my ears naturally heard it in a negative way.

When I looked up, the girl with the purple backpack was smiling at me. Her black hair had one green streak in it and gently brushed against the top of a camera she had dangling around her neck. She had deep, brown, curious eyes that matched her skin.

"I really do love it," she continued. "It's really unique, and it's really serious looking. It says, 'Look out world, I'm a professional writer!! Everything that crosses paths with me can and will be used as writing material!' You have a superpower."

My heart sank. How could she reach inside of my soul like that in a matter of seconds? I took a big gulp and mustered up the courage to reply.

"Hi. Yeah, my mom got it for me for my birthday." I smiled, probably weirdly.

"That's cool. For my last birthday my mom got me a used turntable and a few accessories for my camera. I'm Abbie, by the way. That's *A-B-B-I-E*. My pronouns are she/her."

I didn't know why she was telling me this. Did she tell everyone?

"I'm Gabriela . . ." I fanned through my journal. Then I asked: "Not to be rude but are you in middle school? You look way younger. Also, why did you tell me the 'she/her' thing?"

"I didn't know we were playing twenty questions, but I'm game. Answer number one: I skipped a grade, and this is literally my first day. I was out for a month, um, sick. Answer number two: because those are my pronouns and I want people to use my pronouns. Period." Abbie kneeled down to *actually* tie her shoe.

"Why would anyone use different pronouns?" I said curiously.

"It's not good to assume you know someone's pronouns just by looking at them. It sucks to have someone decide who you are based on how you look. Ya know? Maybe I'm genderfluid and my pronouns are they/them or ze/zir! Point is, don't assume and just . . . ASK! Es fácil; C'est facile!" She finished and popped up from the ground.

"I guess I never really thought much about it," I said, playing with my backpack straps. I wasn't sure what half of those words meant, but I didn't want to sound like I didn't know anything, especially something as important as this. "Well, I think it's really cool you spell your name *A-B-B-I-E*. I've never heard of it being spelled *A-B-B-I-E* before."

"Just because you haven't heard of it doesn't make it less real or valid."

She had a point.

"Valid," I said as we both smiled and walked toward the school entrance.

5

Abbie and I parted ways to homeroom, and I walked through the door of room 202 ten minutes early to see Mrs. Andersen inspecting and tending to her flowers as usual. While she buzzed like a bee visiting her flowers, I cleared my throat and asked her, "What does *queer* mean?"

She looked into the distance as if I had asked the hardest question in the world, then finally said, softly, "Well, when I was growing up . . ."

Oh great . . . Here we go . . .

She continued, "*Queer* had a different meaning when I was a kid. It was a word used to be mean or make fun of someone. But I think, now, it's being used differently. *Queer* is another word for *gay* or being LGBT-plus. But I'm not part of that community nor am I a professional or expert in that community, so I don't want to tell you something that may not be true or authentic." She said this with intention. She said it with passion. I respected that.

Even though I wasn't expecting her to know everything in the universe, I was happy to find out that maybe *queer* wasn't *bad*. But when Jonathan had said it to me, it had felt bad. I didn't know why someone would call me that. I didn't think of myself as being queer.

I slid my bag onto my desk and pulled out my book to read.

"Is that all that was on your mind?" Mrs. Andersen gently asked.

"Yeah. I'm good." I stayed frozen to the pages of my book, even though my eyes weren't reading any of the words.

"All right, well, I'm here. All day! You know where to find me." She finished with a welcoming voice and walked over to her desk.

I peered over my book, trying to see the expression on her face. People are usually good at controlling their face during a discussion, but after, your face relaxes and reveals more. Her face stayed neutral. She must have felt me watching her.

Before the bell for homeroom rang, I quickly excused myself and rushed to my safe place.

When I got to the library, I beelined to my favorite corner. I sat down and took a deep breath. Like a breath of calm waves coolly rushing to the ocean, my fast-beating heart began to beat at a peaceful pace. My cheeks started to feel less warm. I closed my eyes, took a deep breath, and my daydream reappeared. I let my body float on a foam of teal water. I thought about how light I felt. And even though I still couldn't see what I looked like, I knew how I felt.

Free.

The window in the library was slightly cracked open and perfumed the room with beautiful blooming flowers.

I was home.

My daydream never lasts too long, so my mind was on to the next thought soon enough. I thought about how humiliating it would be for someone to read my own words. I decided I would write a fake draft of my essay. It would be a stand-in for the real thing. It would be personal but not personal. I cracked open my journal, folded the real essay pages back, quickly peered around making sure no one was looking, and started a new piece.

Gabriela Alicia Ricci

Mrs. Andersen: English, Teal

1 October 2021

My Authentic Self

I know who I am. It's other people who are too obsessed with themselves to care about who I am.

No. That's bad. Ugh, and I guess sorta mean.

Gabriela Alicia Ricci

Mrs. Andersen: English, Teal

1 October 2021

My Authentic Self

I am smart. I am kind. I am important.

Noooope, that's definitely from a movie.

Gabriela Alicia Ricci

Mrs. Andersen: English, Teal

1 October 2021

My Authentic Self

I don't know.

That'll do. That's pretty truthful!

The first bell rang, and I booked it to English. I weaved past the clambering sound of students with full stomachs not wanting to go back to class. As I neared room 202, I caught a glimpse of Maya.

No.Must.Not.Get.Distracted.

While people were busy having their own separate conversations, and Maya was far enough away not to notice, I slipped into the classroom before she could get close. Even though she was in my class, I made an effort to sit in front of her so there was no possibility of my attention drifting.

As students trickled in, I peered over heads. Had someone seriously taken my seat? Oh, of course Jonathan did. I was only four minutes late. My seat was the best. I mean, it was essentially the window seat on the plane. I could get lost in my self-made cocoon while still having access to nature. It was the best of both worlds. I slunk into the second-best seat in class in the third row and took a breath. This was it. Time to share our essay drafts.

6

As I got my things organized, I looked up and noticed everyone was still having their own private conversations. I cracked my neck and grabbed onto my pen nervously. Finally, Mrs. Andersen passed back our quizzes from last week and began to talk about what was on the agenda today. I popped a piece of gum in and chewed recklessly.

"Hey, chompers, wanna share?" Jonathan demanded, flipping his e-boy hair out of his face. He held out his hand.

I unclenched my fist from my hoodie pocket and gave him two pieces.

"That's what I thought." He laughed loudly, looking around for a reaction. The classroom hooted.

Mrs. Andersen stopped talking.

The classroom held their breath like everyone was keeping a secret.

"I didn't realize this was an episode of *Bring the Funny*, Mr. Kazilonas. Next time, maybe bring it." Mrs. Andersen continued.

"Oooooo!!!" the class roared.

"All right, settle down."

"Whatever," Jonathan scoffed and turned back to his seat and his phone under the desk.

"What are you looking at, weirdo?" I heard a voice say a minute later. I could feel eyes on me. I didn't look up. It wasn't hard to figure out it was Jonathan.

Without replying I shoved my hand farther into my hoodie pocket.

Oblivious to what had just happened, Mrs. Andersen announced that she would be pairing us up and hoped everyone had finished a draft of their essay, since we'd be critiquing our partners. Partnering up for an activity should be abolished. Nothing good ever comes of it.

And ooof course there was an odd number in class today so I didn't have a partner. I noticed Abbie in the back of the class, but she already had one. She gave me a smile and head nod. I smiled back. I guess I should have jumped on the opportunity to be her partner sooner. Oh well. I guess I didn't mind. I would just have to critique my own essay. This was actually perfect. I started writing in my journal. Head down, really going at it. Hard at work. Blending in. Yep. Nothing to see here. No one would notice I didn't have a partner.

As soon as Mrs. Andersen noticed I was riding solo, she came up to me and said she'd be my partner.

I think this may be worse than having a partner.

"So, let's see what you've got, Gabriela."

"It's not any good," I said, smiling hesitantly.

I pulled out my notebook and flipped past my folded pages, then flipped back and opened them. I was going to show her my real first draft. I was at terms with having to work with Mrs. Andersen. Plus, she was a teacher; she'd give the best feedback

"All right! Let's see what you have . . . I'm excited to read your work."

"Oh, thank you. I don't know really what I'm doing, to be honest."

"We all don't really know what we are doing . . . to be honest." She smirked.

I held back a smile but hoped she could see it in my eyes.

Mrs. Andersen reached over to see my draft and started reading. I doodled on another piece of paper.

"Mmm . . ." I heard her say audibly. As her eyes grazed each one of my words.

I started doodling faster.

Before she could make any more sounds, Mrs. Andersen looked toward the door. I could only see the top of the person's head waiting outside the door; it looked like a student, not an adult.

The class was not paying attention, but I watched every movement. Mrs. Andersen gleefully opened the door and smiled and guided the student to the front of the classroom.

"Everyone, this is Héctor Gomez! He just moved here from Arizona! Let's all welcome Héctor!" Some of the class slow clapped, while others were still totally unaware of a new student entering our classroom. Jocelyn, in the second row, was applying lipstick for the thirty-eighth time today, when she accidentally dropped it. Héctor came to her rescue and picked it up. He smiled when their eyes met. I was going to be sick.

Héctor had warm brown skin, dark almond eyes, jet-black hair, and a beauty mark on the left side of his chin. His bangs covered only one eye, and he wore charcoal eyeliner. He was beautiful.

I cracked my neck, reorganized my desk, and prayed I wasn't going to have to partner with him. I mean, how could we be partners? He'd been here, like, three seconds and didn't even have an essay I could critique.

"Héctor, why don't you partner up with Gabriela?" Mrs. Andersen motioned Héctor to join me at my table. "Isn't that perfect!" she said cheerfully.

Héctor pulled up a seat and started using his pencils as drumsticks at the edge of his desk. I studied him for a moment.

This dude was dark. I could just imagine him saying to his parents: "It's not a phase!" Also, who uses pencils? So weird.

I loved it.

"I'm Gabriela. I know you don't have an essay and it's supposed to be a partner essay critique. So, honestly, it's your lucky day. We won't do it at all. I'm totally chill with that." I hoped he wasn't going to object to this amazing offer.

I waited for him to reply, but he didn't.

I said again, "Listen, dude, we don't have to do this. I'm sure my essay would bore you anyway."

Héctor smiled but still didn't reply.

I tried again. "We don't have—"

"Chill. I heard you. I was thinking we looked like we could be siblings. Are you Guatemalan too?"

I gulped.

No. I wasn't.

I wanted to tell him I was adopted and I wished I had a brother who looked like me—or anyone in my family that looked like me. I wanted to tell him that he was the closest thing I saw to seeing myself. I was Honduran, but I'd never met anyone from Honduras. The closest I'd been to Honduras was the tag on my shirt: HECHO EN HONDURAS.

But if I told him that, maybe he would feel sorry for me, or think I was making a generalization. Assuming we were the same when we weren't.

Luckily he continued, and I didn't have to respond.

"Honestly, I am surprised at how there's only a few of us BIPOC kids here. This is not how I pictured Brooklyn." He bit at his black painted nails.

"What's BIPOC?"

"Black, Indigenous, People of Color, homie. But forreal, you could be Lenca."

"Oh, yeah, I knew that, sorry. Yeah, it's weird. Probably because this is a more gentrified community."

"Ah, yes, systemic racism and income inequality, I know all about it." Now he was biting off the black nail polish from his nails.

"So . . . ," I started, trying to switch topics, "the truth is I don't really want to share my essay."

"I see. I get it. It's probably personal. What if I told you something super personal about me?" Héctor asked, leaning in. "Would that make you more comfortable?"

"I guess?" I said, confused but fascinated.

"I'm bisexual." He blurted it out with complete ease.

"Oh. Okay. That's super personal. That's great. Congratulations," I said, tipping an imaginary hat.

He laughed. "Are you freaked out or something?"

"No, not really. What do you want me to do? Throw you a party? I know plenty of bisexual people." Well, not plenty, but a couple.

"Ha ha, a party. I love it, dude. You're funny. That's cool. Do you know Josh, by any chance?"

"What. No? Maybe?" I said nervously.

"I'm messing with you. People seem to think all LGBTQIA+ people know each other. Eh, guess it kinda can be true sometimes. Not many of us can be visible, and when we are we form a community."

"Oh, I definitely don't think that at all," I said, hoping my beads of sweat from my forehead weren't visible. *What did the* IA *stand for?* I thought to myself.

"So anyway, you gonna let me read your essay?"

"Wow, slow down, Héctor, we *just* met."

We both laughed, and our sighs collided with the ringing of the last bell.

7

W hen I got to my last period before gym, I felt a sense of relief because:

1. None of the snarky, annoying people from homeroom, or any of my classes for that matter, were in this particular class.

2. It was an advanced Spanish class, and I was the only Hispanic person there. This was my moment to shine, baby.

3. It's the last real class of the day.

4. My Spanish teacher was so nice.

5. I get to see Maya again and maybe even impress her with my Spanish.

Mrs. Dickens was a very eager teacher. Passionate and kind, but eager. She was sporting crooked glasses with smudged lenses, an old-school blowout, and bright-orange blouse. Her fingerprints smeared across her green smoothie-shaker bottle looked like a crime scene. She was awesome.

We were starting our family unit today. Though at first glance Mrs. Dickens may have given off an uncool vibe, she would always introduce a new unit with a clip from a current TV show or movie. This time we were going to watch *One Day at a Time* on Pop TV. But before the show loaded up, there was a knock at the door. I could only imagine who was behind it.

Mrs. Dickens had this ongoing skit she would do, where she would pretend to be an older woman from Spain or a different Spanish speaker from another country, so she could show us regional differences in Spanish. Oh, and get this, she would also play herself. A back and forth, literal jumping from one side of the room to the other, playing two parts. So anyway, each scene began with a knock at the door, and we were all anxious to see who would be stopping by this time.

The knock continued with a rhythm to it.

Bum dum da dum dum . . . bum bum (or whatever sound a very elaborate knock makes).

"Quién esssss?" Mrs. Dickens said dramatically, with a raised eyebrow and half-cracked crooked smile.

The door opened, and a girl dramatically exclaimed: "Soy yo! Abbie!" Arms raised up and body posed like a gymnast who'd stuck the landing.

Everyone burst out laughing. Even Mrs. Dickens seemed quite impressed.

"Ay, qué linda. I almost forgot you were coming today. Maybe because you're ten minutes late?" She spoke with a grin, but honesty trickled from her face.

"Lo siento, Señora Dickens. I was caught up doing something fabulous somewhere, you wouldn't know the place, but I promise you it was fantastical. Anyway, I'm here now. You're welcome!"

"Well, after that entrance, I think Elena Alvarez may have some competition in the drama department." The class laughed.

Mrs. Dickens started to introduce Abbie, but Abbie decided to take the lead.

"Hi, everyone. I'm Abbie. That's A-B-B-I-E. I know I look young for my age. I'll drop my skincare routine later."

The class roared.

"All right, Abbie," Mrs. Dickens said, gesturing to Abbie to sit. "All right, siéntate, por favor."

Abbie took her time and finally plopped herself a row behind me. The classroom chatter softly faded as soon as Mrs. Dickens hit the lights and played *One Day at a Time*.

"Oh my god, Abbie, what are you doing here? Your entrance was more dramatic than Abuelita's opening credits." We both laughed at the screen.

I continued, "That's awesome that you're in a class with me! Hopefully this class isn't too hard. It's advanced Spanish." I was almost jumping out of my seat with excitement.

"Well, I was taking French for the last year and I'm pretty much fluent. I decided it was time to switch it up." She said this with a hair flip, while casually showing off her glittery nails. She leaned in closer and whispered with excitement: "I want to be a polyglot!"

When Abbie spoke it was like a monologue, but one that was engaging. No snores in the back row or tomatoes thrown at her. When she spoke, the world listened. I mean, the way she entered class.

Like she wanted to be seen.

Like she was proud to be seen.

After a few seconds in la-la-land I snapped out of it and whispered back: "A what-a-what?"

She smiled, reached into her bag, and took a bite out of a Luna Bar like she was chewing off a piece of overdone steak. She took a deep breath. She picked up the soft crumbs that had fallen onto our table one by one with her pinky finger, smooshed them together, and ate them. Then she said, "It means you can speak multiple languages. One day, you know, when I'm a photojournalist for *National Geographic*, I want to be able to go to any country and speak their language—you know, after I'm finishing DJ'ing a Boiler Room set en Rio de Janeiro."

I'd never really thought about learning a language for any purpose other than getting a good grade. I'd never even heard of the word *polyglot*. It sounded too similar to *blood clot*, but I could dig it.

After a moment of silence—and it only took a moment for her to inhale her Luna Bar—I turned to Abbie and said, "That's so cool. I mean, words in general. I never even heard of the word *polyglot*. But I always wondered if there was a word for knowing a lot of languages. It's so cool how thoughts or feelings can equal a word, but sometimes you don't have a word for it yet. Language really is interesting."

She nodded her head in agreement. Her teeth and braces glistened in the dark.

"Yeah, totally. I love learning new vocabulary. I learn it mostly for myself, but it's helped me be able to explain who I am." Her voice faded out.

I saw Abbie look down anxiously and wipe the remains of her bar from the table and onto the floor. Even though she'd stopped speaking, I knew there was more she wasn't saying. I could see it in the absence of words.

"I get what you mean," I said. Even though I didn't know if I did.

"Ladies. Silencio, por favor. Pueden hablar más tarde."

Ladies. I felt my skin crawl.

Before the show ended, I excused myself to go to the bathroom. Mrs. Dickens handed me the hall pass card that read *señoritas* in bright pink letters, and I shoved it into my back pocket. As I walked down the hallway, I stopped at the fountain to get a drink. Reaching for the lever, I noticed my gym teacher, Mr. Philbrook, walking by and staring at me. Then I heard him clear his throat. If clearing your throat was a language, I would have been fluent in it. I stood up.

He looked down at my hall pass and cleared his throat again.

"Gabriela, remember, you have to have your hall pass *on* you at all times."

"Um. It is?"

"You know what I mean. Please put it around your neck. We didn't dip into the school budget to buy beautiful lanyards for no one to use."

I took a deep breath, grabbed the hall pass out of my back pocket, and placed it around my neck. I shot Mr. Philbrook a fake smile.

"Atta girl. See you next period."

8

So, here's the thing. I don't dislike Mr. Philbrook. I don't even dislike gym. *Dislike* is such a strong word for me, and I don't have the energy to house that type of feeling in my body. But I love gym and I love sports. I'm actually pretty good at sports. I just think that some of his activities are a bit . . . outdated. For example, the other day we played capture the flag. Is it 1830? Are we at war? I mean, yeah, I guess the country is always at war, and it's middle school— it's pretty brutal out here—but is it necessary to have a sport that promotes a literal battlefield?

To be honest, I didn't really have any feelings about gym until the beginning of the year. I started to get super uncomfortable undressing in front of the girls in the locker room. This was for two reasons: 1) I didn't really want them to see my body.

Wait, there's three reasons: 1) I didn't really want them to see my body. 2) I didn't want to see my body. 3) I didn't want anyone thinking I was looking at them in that sort of setting.

Today was going to be a typical gym class, except instead of Mr. Philbrook's outdated games, we were doing a softball scrimmage. We hadn't chosen teams yet, but I wasn't really worried. I was a good hitter so people tended to choose me.

"Boys and girls, line up. Line up! Line up! Toes behind the red line!" Mr. Philbrook howled through the screeching of his whistle.

"I wanna see two lines. Boys in one line. Girls in the other line." His voice grew impatient.

Everyone started scurrying to get a place in their line.

I had done this a million times, but today I found myself standing in the middle.

Frozen.

Finally, Lucy waved me over. I followed her to the girls' line.

I looked up and saw that Héctor was watching me from the other line. He smiled. I smiled back.

I wondered what he thought of me now.

9

I did a good job avoiding Héctor for the rest of gym and the rest of school. I didn't really want to talk about how uncomfortable I felt in gym. I didn't even know if he knew I felt uncomfortable.

"Gabriela, wait up."

As I walked out of the building that afternoon, I heard an out-of-breath voice calling my name. I put in my earbuds, turned up the volume, and walked faster.

"Hey, Gabriela. What's up? I feel like you've been avoiding me," Héctor said, finally catching up to me.

"Oh, no. I-I'm . . . I mean. I just need to get home. I'm not avoiding you."

"I've known you all of forty-two seconds, and I already can tell when you're not being completely honest," Héctor smirked at me.

"I'm sorry. I just felt like it was awkward in gym today." I pulled out my earbuds and held them in my sweaty palms.

"How?"

"I mean . . ."

"What? You can talk to me, if you want . . ."

"I guess . . . I feel embarrassed to say it."

"That's okay. You don't have to say anything."

"Well, now you're making me want to say it, ha ha."

"I do have that effect!"

"I mean, didn't you see me just freeze when Mr. Philbrook told us to get in line?"

"I guess . . ."

"You're being nice. I totally froze. I don't really know why . . . I just didn't know what line I wanted to be in. And maybe I've been on autopilot all of these years and never thought too much about it or I pushed it way down inside even when it did make me uncomfortable. Ah, sorry. You probably think I sound ridiculous. I mean, why would that be a difficult choice. I'm a girl, you're a boy. The end." I finished, and tried not to start crying.

"Hey, no, no wait. Not the end. It's not ridiculous. I can understand how it could be a difficult decision. And for the record, that's not how I identify. I'm more genderfluid and I'm okay with any pronouns, and I don't know how you identify because you've never said."

I stood frozen again. This time, I turned around so Héctor couldn't see me.

Héctor placed his hand on my shoulder. "Gabriela. It's okay not to know."

I whipped around, tears running down my face now. "Then why do you know? Why does it seem like it's so easy for you?!"

"It hasn't always been easy . . . Trust me. Sometimes, it's easier to look like I've got everything together, when I don't. Plus, I wasn't always this confident. It took a while. Don't put so much pressure on yourself."

"Thanks, Héctor."

"De nada! Can I hug you?" he asked with his arms open and ready for a hug.

"Ha. Yes. Permission granted." I unclenched my arms and hugged him.

"Funny!

"I guess I have that effect."

Héctor stepped back from our hug and continued, "Do you want me to talk to Mr. Philbrook?"

"And say what?" I replied through my tears.

"And say, we're gonna kick his binary-thinking butt if he doesn't let us just choose our teams!"

"Sure. I'd like that. Thanks for being there for me." I let out a small side smile and could feel a sense of pride expand from inside of me. Proud to know Héctor. Proud to start learning about me.

10

When I got to school the next day, Héctor met me at my locker and told me that Mr. Philbrook didn't care at all. He said we could choose our teams as long as the numbers were even.

The anxiety that had been swimming through my veins started to disappear. I felt a thousand times lighter. Gym was going to be fun again.

The week flew by, and it was awesome having two new people in my life who accepted me. I saw Héctor and Abbie at the beginning of the day and Héctor at the end. Everything in between didn't bother me as much. My run-ins with Jonathan didn't feel as big since I had back-up now. Plus, it seemed like he was keeping his distance a little more. Being alone was super bait for bullies.

◎ ◎ ◎

It was already Sunday when I realized I'd been reading almost all weekend. And when my brain got overwhelmed with reading, I would write.

~illusions~

I feel like I'm floating between
space and time.
s p a c e
TIME.
The way the world sees me is not how
I see me or how I feel. But I—
Don't really even know how I feel (yet).

On Sundays, my mom and I usually went out for breakfast, to the local music store, and then to the farmers market. At breakfast we would order two completely different meals and split it. When our stomachs no longer ached for pancakes, we'd go to Jupiter. Not the planet. That was the name of the music store. But it might as well have been its own planet. There was no place on earth like it. We would dig through old records and CDs and then pick our top four to buy. When we would meet at the counter there would always be at least two that were the same. It was pretty amazing being on the same wavelength—or should I say, .WAVlength.

Before I fully opened my eyes in bed, I heard the buzzing sound of the Grateful Dead. *"Wake up to find out that you are the eyes of the world . . ."* I heard a non–Grateful Dead member humming up the stairs. The humming sound invited morning visitors in the form of cats.

My mom stood in my doorway with coffee in her hand and her hair still wet from her shower, singing.

"Time to wake up, flower child. Breakfast is singing our names!"

I took out my night guard and rubbed the sleepy eyes out of my corners and headed to the bathroom.

"Shower power! Pew! Pew! Pew!" Mom said in a high-pitched, singsongy voice.

When we got to Betty's Diner, cars were packed in like sardines. Betty's was literally one of the only places in our Brooklyn neighborhood that had mini parking across the street.

"We've got this," my mom said, kissing her amethyst necklace.

We did. We always got parking.

When we were seated, I ordered a hot chocolate and my mom ordered decaffeinated coffee. We studied the menu like we were studying for the most important exam of our life. Moments passed, we peered over our oversized menus, and I said: "Pancakes and eggs?"

"Yes! You know how I have a sweet tooth. You can handle the egg situation. I trust you." My mom high-fived me.

I practically had the menu memorized but hoped that maybe their specials today had the exact combination of ingredients I liked. I didn't want to seem like I was demanding of certain ingredients. I'd watched how some servers walked away from a table and went back to the kitchen and the line cook would raise their eyebrows.

Unsuccessful, I put down the menu and decided to create my own scramble. Avocado, chorizo, onions, green peppers—no, no onions because my mom doesn't like onions. And pepper jack cheese. Always pepper jack cheese.

After we finished breakfast, we were off to Jupiter. When we pulled up to the store, I saw a kid around my age outside, arguing with an adult—or it appeared to be arguing. I couldn't make out what they were saying or who the boy was since the man was towering over him.

My mom glanced over to me and said, "You know it isn't polite to stare! Let's get going. I think I'm in a jazz mood? Let's see what finds us."

As I walked through the doors and into the familiar aisles of music, it was as if I was walking through my own musical. I let myself be mesmerized by the birdsong of voices that had made a historical imprint on the lives of so many. I was swept away, imagining people dancing Brazilian bossa nova from the greats, Caetano Veloso and Gal Costa. The colorful sounds of Marisa Monte radiated throughout the overly stocked shelves. I danced to "Mighty Sparrow," fell onto my knees playing imaginary air saxophone to "Roaring Lion." Other than the library, the music store was one of my havens.

When I had finished my musical number, I looked up and saw the guy my age who'd been arguing outside standing at the end of the aisle. It looked like he was putting away CDs. I went closer, and my heart started beating faster, realizing it was Héctor. I started to back up slowly, then tripped. I wasn't sure I wanted Héctor to meet my mom because I liked being Héctor's pretend sibling. If he saw my mom, maybe he would think I wasn't really Hispanic and we could never really be siblings.

He looked up.

"Whoa, slow down there, killer. Were you trying to back away slowly like that Simpson's GIF?"

I felt my face rising with redness.

"Oh, no, I was just. Yeah . . . you got me. Simpson's GIF. Is it JIF or GIF? Does anyone know?" I dusted myself off and pretended to ask customers as they walked by.

"There's two things I don't talk about at work," Héctor shot back with an effortlessly beautiful smile. "Politics—because don't test me—and the correct way to say GIF."

"Ha ha. Well, anyway . . ." I said awkwardly. Most things I said were awkward. I'm awkward. I'm so in-my-head awkward, it's like when words come out of my mouth it astonishes me—

"What are you doing here?" I asked, looking around to make sure my mom wasn't nearby.

"Honestly? I stole, like, fifty CDs, put them in a crate, and hauled my way back home. Then I felt guilty and came back to restock them in their respective genres," Héctor said seriously.

"Dude, that's horrible. We have to tell someone. Or pay for them. I don't even—"

Héctor cut me off. "Chill, dude. I'm joking!" He looked directly into my eyes and smiled.

I sighed with relief. Wow, maybe I did need to chill. *Do I need to chill? Anyone, anyone?*

"I work here. My dad is the new franchise owner, and I thought it was time I got paid for my labor. So, here I am, restocking music—un-stolen music—as a paid employee. What about you, Gabs, what are you up to?"

Wait. Did he just call me Gabs? And did he say *franchise?* My mom was going to freak. She'd always thought this was a Brooklyn-local indie business.

"I guess I should have put two and two together. I thought I saw you outside . . . argu—talking to an adult or someone, who totally looked like they owned a franchise."

"Aw, you saw that? Yeah, that was my dad. He was upset about my brother. My brother has had a boyfriend for over a year, and my dad found out I met him first. I guess he was hurt, not, like, upset or angry.

I know what you're thinking: Does queer run in the family, or what? Are we just amazing?"

"I think you're all probably just really amazing." I stood up a little taller. "So, does *queer* not offend you?"

"Mm . . . no? Only if someone was using it to purposely be hurtful. Other than that, it's a word to celebrate."

"Yeah . . . I guess I asked someone recently, and they said they weren't even part of the community and they were a teacher, so—"

"Okay. Yeah . . . you have me now. And it's time," Héctor said, pushing his hair out of his eyes. "It's definitely time for some Queer 101. Find me on Monday, or just text me. I'm surprised we haven't exchanged digits yet, actually. Before you ask, nope, I don't have Insta or any social media. It's a weird place. It's so impersonal. Just text me." Héctor grabbed my phone and put his number in.

A dad being upset he didn't meet his son's boyfriend first was family drama? I was still afraid to even admit I might have a crush on a girl. Maya! Maya . . . ah. I had to stop. But I didn't want to stop thinking about her. Maybe I wouldn't.

"So, anyway, sorry about your dad being hurt." I looked down at my Docs, beginning to feel self-conscious about my mismatched shoelaces.

"Yo, don't worry about it. My brother, Arturo, is inviting his boyfriend, David, over for dinner tonight. My idea—I know, I'm full of surprises." He smiled that beautiful, crooked smile again.

"Young man," a voice called out. "Can you help me find Jackson Browne? I looked in the country section and can't seem to find him anywhere. Maybe I should have brought my readers," the woman mumbled to herself.

"Of course I can. Why don't you follow me? Oh, I just love that color on you . . ."

Héctor led the older lady down the streaming aisles of music magic, reaching down and grabbing every single Jackson Browne CD. He talked about each track on the album like he'd produced every one. As if he had transported himself back to the '70s and sat in the studio with Jackson. Their voices were fading into the distance when I heard my mom say, "Let's get out of here. I don't want to get to the farmers market too late. You know how crowded it gets. Wanna share what you got?"

We both had chosen Gal Costa. We decided on her, Gilberto Gil, and Cateano Veloso. On our ride to the farmers market, my mom lowered the music and asked: "So, who was that handsome kid you were talking to? Does he have a name? Deets."

Did my mom just say *deets*? Cringe. But I still loved her.

"Oh, that's Héctor. He just moved here from Arizona, and he's helping his dad out at the store. His dad—well, I don't know how to tell you this. You may want to sit down."

"Sweetie, we are in a car. We are both sitting down. Literally. Just tell me."

"Okay, so . . . Héctor's dad is the franchise owner of this store. The store is a franchise. I just Googled it too. There's about a dozen of them. I'm sorry you had to find out this way." I rested my hand on her shoulder.

"I always thought it was a local business—whatever will I do?!" my mom cried dramatically.

"Wait, so are you not upset, or just processing this in a really . . . unexpected way?" I asked without blinking.

"Of course I'm not upset. If this upset me, then I'm in trouble. Life's too short. Plus, it's even better:

now we can support your cute new friend and his family."

She looked at me cheerfully as we pulled up to an open parking space.

11

When we got home, I helped my mom unpack the groceries. She was quiet, but her energy still seemed light. I felt like I could leave her alone for a bit and she'd be all right. I told her I needed to finish some homework and bolted to my room. I closed the door halfway, jumped onto my bed, cracked my neck and opened up my laptop.

I searched *LGBTQIA* online first. I knew what LGBTQ was, I just didn't know enough about the *I* and *A*.

I read the first result:

The letters LGBTQIA refer to Lesbian, Gay, Bisexual, Transgender, Queer or Questioning, Intersex, and Asexual or Allied.

I had no clue what *intersex* or *asexual* were. I guessed it was time to take the plunge into the black hole of YouTube. I typed in "intersex" in the search bar first. A video labeled "I'm Intersex and Transgender" popped up. I watched the video a couple times.

> "Trans *means you don't identify as your sex assigned at birth. Sex and gender aren't the same thing. Both sex and gender are on a spectrum. It is estimated that one out of two hundred people are born intersex, which is the same statistic as naturally born* redheads. Intersex *describes people whose biology doesn't fit the typical definition of* male *or* female."

I clicked on more videos to learn about the experiences of other intersex people. As I clicked, I remembered that there was a show I had watched where a character was intersex. I felt like even though there still weren't enough shows on TV about the wide range of other people who identified as LGBT+, there were more shows about them than intersex people. I wished there were more shows that had intersex characters. I let the next video load and the next and next. Yep, I had entered the YouTube vortex. Next time, I should grab some snacks.

As the tenth video or eleventh—who knows, I lost count—loaded, I saw it was titled "How I Came Out: My Intersex and Trans Journey."

I stuck my hands into my hoodie and felt something crunchy. Could it be? No, it couldn't be. It could. Kale chips! Now I was totally prepared for the black hole. When I looked up, I saw a girl maybe a couple years younger than me talking about being born intersex and realizing that she felt more like a girl. She looked familiar, like I had seen her on TV before. I looked at her subscriber count: 300,000. I paused the video and started scrolling through her channel to find her most recent post.

Oh.

My.

God.

It was Abbie!

I had a kale chip probably permanently stuck to the roof of my mouth and still couldn't get over the fact that I had found Abbie's YouTube channel. It was public. It's not like it was an invasion of privacy, right? Why hadn't she told me? I mean why would she? I definitely felt like we were becoming friends, but we'd just met. She was a legit YouTuber and hadn't even told me? There were even clips of her being interviewed on the *Today* show. Should I tell her I saw her channel tomorrow at school? Like, oh, hey, just randomly found your channel and watched every video you posted, not weird at all.

Before I could click the next video, my mom yelled from the bottom of the stairs.

"Dinner's ready! I just picked some delicious spinach from the garden. Janet told me to pick as much as I can before the bugs got to it. It's, like, two bags' worth and pretty near perfect."

I slowly closed my laptop and ran downstairs.

12

After dinner, I helped my mom clean the dishes and went back to my room while she went back to finishing her quilt for our cousin's baby. My mom had her own personal hobbies, most of which didn't include checking in on me. She checked in on me the perfect amount, though.

Instead of going back on YouTube, I laid in bed and stared at my ceiling. I could still see the marks the glow-in-the-dark star stickers made, even after we'd taken them down. I shut my eyes and imagined the stars were still there.

A loud ping startled me. It was a Facebook alert. I thought I had deleted the app months ago, when I'd found out my entire family had signed up. I saw them enough in real life. I unlocked my phone and discovered I had two notifications from Maya. I hadn't spoken to her, really, since elementary school. Although

I felt like we spoke with our eyes sometimes. I know I'm corny. She had liked one of my profile pictures from a while back. What was she doing deep-liking my pictures?

The first time I'd met Maya was in first grade. I was tripping over feelings for her. While this boy, Charlie, was bringing me gifts and playing it off as something friends do, I only had one thing on my mind. Maya.

The first time I think she really saw me was when I was holding the door for everyone coming back in from recess. This is how eager I was: a teacher didn't even assign me to hold it; I volunteered as a way to see her. It took sixty-seven people to pass me, and it was worth the wait. She was the most beautiful girl I had ever seen. When our eyes met, I felt that if she was the last person I ever saw, I wouldn't mind—she was the only one I wanted to be seen by. She brushed by me and was the only one to say thank you for holding the door.

The next few years we were in class together, and I'd felt my heart flying. She even said one time in a yearbook that we were friends. I felt embarrassed for even remembering that and clinging to it because maybe she just said that to everyone. We didn't hang outside of school, but school friends worked for me. Then, when we all got older and everyone was saying they were dating someone in their friend group, she came back from winter break and announced she had a boyfriend named Sam, who she'd met on vacation.

When we got to middle school, Maya announced that she had another boyfriend, who she met in France during the summer. Jessie, who used to be Maya's best friend, figured out that Maya had lied and this French boy didn't exist. She found her finsta and then compared it with her public account and found out she didn't even go to France. Jessie is the type of friend—or, I guess, person—who will find out the truth, at anyone's expense. She was in the business of exposing people. The only recent photos that Maya was tagged in on her finsta were with a girl. There were pictures of them holding hands and pictures tagged of them together. I never really looked because I never felt like it was my business. When Jessie found out, she spread it faster than a new iPhone software update. She went out of her way to humiliate Maya.

Anyway, ever since then, no one looked at Maya the same. It wasn't because she was a lesbian, but because people felt she wasn't upfront with her friends and couldn't trust them.

Last week, I heard that Maya had just officially broken up with her on-and-off again girlfriend, Lucy. I had never dated anyone before. But the feeling I felt for Maya must mean I wanted to date her, right? Maybe?

I plunged headfirst into dreamland with Maya on my mind.

13

The next morning, I woke to the curious sun peeking through my pink silk embroidered curtains. The pink created a gorgeous hue that warmly took space inside even the darkest parts of my room.

This morning was different; I felt it in my bones. No humming to made-up songs, no bold back-up singing, no Amy, no Carole. Just silence. The only sound was the color of pink.

This aching silence wasn't something new. My mom goes through periods of managing and then crashes into a deep sea of depression. I did my best to swim with her. Except we're not always swimming; sometimes it feels like we're drowning.

My mom had been seeing a therapist in the city. She'd been going to her for years, longer than I'd been alive. I couldn't even imagine what it would be like knowing someone for longer than I'd been alive.

I remember the first time I asked my mom where she went every Tuesday at 8:00 p.m. I remember the exact time because that's when *Raven's Home* was on. That's when she told me that she went to see someone to talk to about her depression. It felt like such a big and scary word. My mom told me that sometimes it does feel big and scary but going to someone to talk made it better. To be seen, to be witnessed, to be gently heard and cared for in a way that didn't feel like she was handing off a responsibility for feeling the way she felt. When she came back from her therapy appointments, she really did seem better.

But over the last summer, her therapist moved across the country, and my mom is a face-to-face type of gal, and isn't into teletherapy, so she still hadn't found someone she truly connected with.

I worried.

I worried all the time.

I wanted to be enough.

I wanted to be enough to make my mom not depressed anymore.

I stretched my hands to the ceiling, took a big yawn, and rolled out of bed. The smell of Peruvian coffee mixed with the sweet stylings of Laura Nyro's

"Gonna Take a Miracle" might not get my mom out of bed, but it was a way I showed her I was here. That was what she always said to me: "Just be here."

While I was making coffee and feeding the cats, my phone buzzed.

> **HÉCTOR:** Lmk when you're ready for Q101.
> **ME:** Q?
> **HÉCTOR:** Oh, honey, you're so lucky you found me.
> Meet me at the library before homeroom.
> **ME:** I'll be there.

I would be there because that's where I always was, anyway.

Oh, wow. I just realized what Q meant.

I made oatmeal with sliced bananas, mooshed in with just a drizzle of almond butter, and brought it to my mom's room. I grabbed a Nutri-Grain bar for myself.

My mom was going to be in bed for a while, I sensed it, so I took the bus. Normally, she can drive me because she essentially works for herself and makes her own schedule. But when she feels like this, her depression makes her schedule.

I booked it down the street and glided onto the B63 bus down 5th Ave. I texted my mom a cute cat GIF. She didn't reply. When she wasn't in this state she replied the second I hit Send.

Before I could let the feeling of worry consume me, I ran into Abbie as I hopped off. How did she keep magically appearing where I was? *Should I tell her I found her YouTube channel? Is this even as big of a deal as I'm making it? If her identity was a secret, why would she have a channel if she's so private?*

Instead, I told her I was headed to the library to get a lesson in Queer 101. She looked excited, her eyes eager.

I said slowly, "Do . . . you . . . want to come?"

"I thought you'd never ask!" she cried with her hand over her forehead, pretending to crumble to the ground.

When we got to the library it was so early our librarian wasn't even there yet, but the door was open because the school custodian was cleaning.

"Did we get stood up?" Abbie said jokingly.

"Hold up." I quickly called Héctor and waited to hear it ring. I followed the ringing and found him in the back of the library, CD-player headphones on, reading a graphic novel. He was probably the only person I knew who listened to music on a CD player, other than my mom.

"Yo, my bad," he said, lifting one headphone off his ear. "Glad you could make it. Let's get down to business. I pulled a few of my favorite titles of LGBTQIA+ main characters. Now, they're mostly all white, but we gotta work with what we got."

"Wow. Um."

"Dude. I kind of figured you didn't know what LGBTQIA+ was when I brought it up in English. Anyway, books are definitely a way to understand other people's perspectives."

I was silent. I felt my heart trying to leap out of my chest.

"What's more surprising? That I'm not only a master of music but also a book nerd?"

"No, it's not that. I guess this stuff is kind of new to me. My ex-friend—well it's not like we're exes . . . she kind of just moved away, and we don't talk anymore and her mom's a lesbian and moved in with her girlfriend and she doesn't like to—"

I didn't know why I was rambling, or felt so nervous, but I really appreciated Héctor wanting to help me understand. But why did he want me to understand? Did he suspect something about me?

Abbie interjected: "That's super rad. I hope they're in love, treat each other equally in their relationship, and resist any form of discrimination in the toxic misogynistic society we live in! I was just talking about this in my YouTube channel actually. Oh my god, you totally have to subscribe. Blah, long story short, I'm kind of a YouTuber. Like, literally. I get paid. It's boring, I know. Just kidding. I'm in love, I'm in love, and I don't care who knows it!"

"You're a YouTuber? Also, we haven't met yet . . ." Héctor nudged me with his elbow. "I'm Héctor."

"Wow, sorry. Yeah, Abbie, Héctor; Héctor, Abbie. That's awesome, Abbie. I had no idea?" I tried to sound surprised.

"Yeah, I started it a few years ago. My mom spends almost half of each year abroad as a doctor. Right now, she's in Cambodia. I got bored, and my dad—well he's not around as much as he could be. But I know he wants to be? If that makes sense."

"Yeah, I get it. My mom's kind of the same way. When she found out my brother was gay she locked herself in her room for a week. She eventually came around, and when I came out she was genuinely happy for me. But we don't talk about it that much. Does your mom know about your YouTube channel?" Héctor asked.

"Oh my god, of course. She helped me create it. She's been to a few events with me too. My third video went viral. It was definitely unexpected, but my mom was so chill about it."

"What about your dad?" I chimed in awkwardly.

"Honestly, my dad felt like I shouldn't be so public about things. I honestly feel like he doesn't want me to get hurt or be targeted. Being an openly trans girl may come with risks, but it's the way I want to live my life. I don't want to hide who I am. He's also in medicine. An anesthesiologist. Yawn. He puts me to sleep sometimes."

"How do you identify, Héctor?" Abbie asked.

"I'm bisexual, but I'm thinking pansexual feels more authentic to myself. Any pronoun works for me," Héctor replied, without batting an eyelash.

What's pan? I thought to myself as my two new friends formed a friendship in front of me. I was starting to feel invisible. I felt my hands starting to get clammy. I hoped no one was going to ask me how I identified because I had no idea.

"What about you, Gabs?" Abbie asked with a welcoming smile.

"What about me?" I felt my cheeks turn red.

"How do you identify?"

"I'm not sure," I said, shoving my hands into my hoodie so hard I felt my finger go through.

"It's a personal journey," Héctor replied, while squeezing my hand to let me know that he was there.

It was definitely a personal journey—a journey I hadn't even realized I was on. But now that I was on it, I thought I'd keep going.

The bell for homeroom rang—we all began to go our separate ways.

"Hey, Héctor," I called out.

"Yeah?"

"Do you think that the whole gym thing had to do with my identity?"

"Hmm . . . I can't answer that question for you! But I can be someone to talk to. Check out those books. I know that's one place I started when I began questioning my identity."

As soon as Héctor walked away, I ran back to where he'd pulled out those books and checked every single one of them out.

I wanted to learn about other people and their own experiences. I wanted to see myself in these books. I wanted to be seen. I had spent the last few years doing everything to not be seen, but no more.

I was terrified.

But I was ready to do it scared.

14

First to homeroom, I looked around to make sure I was alone. I unzipped my bag and softly slid my fingers down the back of each book spine, reading each title. *Hurricane Child, The Girl From The Sea, The Mighty Heart of Sunny St. James,* and *Melissa.* And a very used *Annie on My Mind.* I touched each book and took in a big sigh, then I slipped my phone from out of my pocket to see if my mom had texted me back. Nothing. She hadn't even read it yet. I was beginning to really worry.

"What are you doing, weirdo?" I heard an unpleasantly familiar voice snarl.

I didn't reply.

One by one, kids streamed into class like a school of fish.

I had two emotions battling with each other. A part of me felt so happy and excited to read the books.

The other part of me was thinking about my mom. I snuck in another text to her from under the table as I sat sardined between Jonathan and his partner in all things mean, Matt.

I ignored them and opened my journal, put in my earbuds, and listened to my playlist *Overthinking* while I sketched until the bell for the next period rang. I scribbled down thoughts, ideas, song names, anything to get me thinking about my English essay and off my mom. Mrs. Andersen would always tell us how important it was to see ourselves in books. She said there's nothing more powerful than writing your story, and that power scares people. That's why half of our reading list is on the banned list—she thinks authors who get banned are rock stars. But why would she push us to write our truths, when the rest of the world wants to ban us when we do?

15

Homeroom was over in the blink of an eye and I didn't exactly feel prepared to keep working on our essays in English. Although I was feeling a lot better about Héctor being my partner, I still wasn't totally comfortable sharing. But sharing wasn't optional.

"So, have you had a chance to check out any of the books I recommended?" Héctor asked as he dragged his chair across the room to join me.

"Kind of," I said quietly.

"Don't sound too excited, Gabs. Ha ha."

"I definitely will soon," I added, trying not to smile. Why was I always hiding how I really felt? I could dance. I could jump out of my seat and do a musical number showing everyone how excited I was to read these books.

"That's cool." Héctor flicked his hair out of his face and quickly changed topics. "So, I have a rough draft of my essay, so now we have to share."

I pressed down on the pages I had folded up and handed him my notebook; he handed me a few pieces of paper.

As I read his essay, I looked out of the corner of my eyes trying to see his reaction to what I had written. Watching made me anxious; not watching made me anxious. So, I did the most rational thing and turned around and continued to read his essay.

I am the son of immigrant parents. I am a brother. I am pansexual. I know who I am because of my life experiences. I know where I am going because I know where I came from. But with all of this said, there were still moments in my life where I questioned who I was. The questions often lead to me not being honest to myself or others. I was afraid to face the answers to these questions.

A time when I wasn't my most authentic self was when I was hiding who I was. I hid because I thought that would make me safe. Hiding didn't protect me. Hiding didn't make me feel safe in my own skin.

I am my most authentic self when I am being the most true version of myself. It is when I am fearless and share myself with others.

Wow. I was amazed at how honest his essay was. I wished I could be that confident.

I turned back around after reading Héctor's essay to see he was already done with mine and listening to music.

When our eyes locked, he slid his headphones down to his neck. "So, let's get to it. The feedback session."

"Okay, sure," I said, my thoughts lingering back to his essay.

"Firstly, I think you have an amazing voice. I can really hear you in this. That's so great. But I don't feel like I see you. Does that make sense?"

"What do you mean?" I tried to say without sounding defensive.

"Well, I mean—don't take this the wrong way, but it's like you're not really getting into it. You're, like, dropping these clues, but not actually telling me who you are."

I didn't know how to reply. Maybe it was because I didn't know who I was. How do you even begin to answer that? *How did you know who you were?*

He continued, "Do you get what I'm saying?"

"Yeah, I get it," I murmured. Just so the conversation could end.

I felt crushed. The first time someone reads my writing, they have that to say to me? I wanted to disappear. I wanted to cry. I wanted to just give up. Writing was the one thing I thought I was good at. Before I could give him his feedback, Mrs. Andersen started talking.

"All right, class," Mrs. Andersen began while flashing the lights on and off, to get our attention. "Does anyone want to share their essay and let the class give notes?"

Why would anyone want to do that? I thought to myself as I slouched in my seat.

"I'll share," Héctor piped up.

"You will?" Mrs. Andersen asked, clearly shocked and excited. "I mean, marvelous!"

After Héctor read his essay, Lucy's hand shot up.

"Yes, Lucy," Mrs. Andersen said.

"My older sister is bisexual. So, like, that's, like, totally cool you are too. When did you know you were, and when did you come out?"

"Let's try to give Héctor feedback instead of asking personal questions," Mrs. Andersen responded firmly.

"Well, to answer your question. I didn't always know. I guess I always was? But I always knew I was different. I came out last year."

"If there's no feedback, we can just go back to silently reading," Mrs. Andersen continued as some sort of weird threat. I would love that.

"I have a question," a voice from the back sounded softly.

"Yes, Maya?" Mrs. Andersen asked, tucking her hair behind her ears.

"How did you become fearless?"

Héctor straightened out his back. "When I got tired of hiding."

Nearly everyone in class was pondering his answer when the bell for block two interrupted our thoughts.

"Sit with me at lunch later?" Héctor asked.

"For sure," I said, gathering my things.

Before I headed to my next class, I straightened out my back and walked toward Maya. She was texting, but I could handle walking over to her when she was on the phone rather than talking to her friends.

"I know this may not help or answer your question," I said slowly, "but I also want to learn how to become fearless. Basically, what I'm saying is . . . you're not alone."

Maya stopped texting and thought it over. "Maybe everything is easier when you know you're not alone."

"Yeah, totally." I could feel my face becoming visibly red.

"See you around," she said with a smirk.

16

I kind of zoned out during Science and Social Studies. I was too happy thinking about how I finally had a friend to sit with at lunch. I was also busy replaying the conversation I'd had with Maya. I felt proud of myself for going up to her and starting the conversation. Even if it wasn't much of a conversation. Maybe I could talk to her more. Maybe she and I could be friends. All I knew was I wanted to be around her. I checked my phone a few times, and my mom had texted me an article about growing your own avocados. I was happy she'd responded, but I wasn't sure how she was feeling. A few moments later, five texts came seconds after one another, all of them different tutorial videos on how to grow an avocado from a seed.

When I finally got to lunch, Héctor was already digging into what appeared to be leftover nachos. I placed my bag down and peered into my lunchbox.

Cobb salad. Minus dressing and a fork. Now I was starting to really worry because silence then rapid texting usually meant something was about to happen. I wasn't sure what, but it made me feel uneasy.

I got in line to grab chipotle ranch and a fork from the salad bar. When I turned to grab the dressing, Maya was standing right behind me. She smiled with her eyes. I smiled a goofy smile.

"Chipotle is the best," she said.

"Yeah, it's pretty up there in terms of salad dressings," I replied nervously. Was this it? Were we talking again? After everyone found out she had lied about having a boyfriend from France, she reinvented herself and stopped talking to everyone she used to talk to. I hadn't really been a close friend, but I was part of her past, so I just got deleted too.

"Ha ha. I forgot how funny you were."

"Yeah, me too."

"Ha ha, see, that right there, that's funny!"

I looked over to see Héctor waving me back to the table while talking to Abbie.

"I better get going," I answered. *I better get going? Why would I say that? Why didn't I ask her to sit with us?*

"Okay, see you later."

I wish. I said that to myself. OR, did I say it out loud?

"I wish, too," she said with a wink.

When I got back to the table, Héctor and Abbie were grinning at me.

"What? Do I have something in my hair? On my face? Real friends tell friends if they have food crammed in their teeth or hair."

"First of all, you haven't even eaten yet, second of all, of course we'd tell you, third of all, what was that about?" Abbie burst out with a curious grin.

"What was *what* about?" I said, trying to keep cool. Key word: *trying.*

"Dude, you're so into her!" Héctor laughed, taking the last bite of his pile of nachos.

"No, I'm not." Lie. "I hardly know her." Lie. "Plus, I'm not a lesbian." Half lie?

"It would be totally cool if you were, Gabriela. We'd still be your friends," Abbie said with a soft nudge.

"Yeah, it's not the eighties."

"I know, but I'm not *into* her. Can we just drop it?"

The excitement from their faces disappeared as they practically nodded in sync.

◎ ◎ ◎

I didn't think I was a lesbian. But, I knew I liked Maya.

"I gotta get going, I'll talk to ya'll later," I tried to say in the least abrupt way possible. I just needed to be alone. I decided to finish lunch in the library. I plopped my things at my favorite table in the back near the window and opened *Annie on My Mind*. Whenever I heard the sound of someone walking by, I quickly hid the title of the book and took a bite out of my salad.

When the bell rang, I started rushing to get to Pre-Algebra and tripped over my bag. As I scurried to shove my books back into it, a hand touched mine.

"What's the rush?"

I looked up and saw Maya kneeling next to me. She had my copy of *Annie on My Mind* cradled in her hands.

I didn't speak.

She did the speaking for both of us.

"I love this book," she said, holding it like precious jewelry. "It's a classic, and it was one of the first books I read when I was coming to terms with being gay."

"I'm not gay," I said.

"I didn't say you were," she replied, with a soothing voice.

"I gotta run, thanks for helping me," I said quickly, taking the book from her hand and getting up.

Our math teacher said that we could either read silently or go to the library once we finished our Pre-Algebra test. I decided to go to the library again before Spanish. I couldn't believe that Maya had read the same book. I quickly turned to the sign-out tab at the back, and sure enough I saw her name.

I wondered who was on her mind when she read the book.

17

When I got to Spanish, Mrs. Dickens was signing in to Netflix. I cleaned the desk I normally sat in and organized my things.

"What are we doing today?" I asked. My being early to every class granted me the insider scoop of the upcoming lesson plan before anyone else.

"We're going to be talking more about friendships and relationships and learning how to be more conversational. We'll split into partners."

What was it with partner activities? Were these teachers trying to make me anxious?

I wanted to say, "Thanks, I hate it," but instead I said, "Sounds great!" Biting on the tip of my pen.

"Whoa, who hurt you?" Abbie asked a couple minutes later as she slid her bag under her desk.

"What?"

"You're chewing on that pen like there's no tomorrow."

"Yeah, whoops, bad habit," I said, still chewing.

"Hey, um . . . you kind of ran away from us today at lunch. You okay?" She tilted her head at me.

"Yeah, I'm fine. I just have a lot on my mind." Like Maya. Like me liking Maya.

"I get it. Well, I'm here if you ever want to talk about it," she said with her welcoming eyes.

"Thanks."

"Buenas tardes, clase," Mrs. Dickens began. "Today we're going to finish up the episode we were on and then break into pairs and practice having a conversation. IN SPANISH! Let's just call it friend-to-friend conversation. Nothing formal. Just a friendly conversation. When your partner is talking, I want you to record three major points they made and vice versa. Entienden?"

"Sí, Señora," the class said in unison.

Mrs. Dickens called out each pair. Abbie was with Josh. Alana was with Angel. Jessica was with Lucy. Finally, I heard my name.

Gabriela y Maya.

I perked up from my chair.

When the episode was finished and the lights turned back on, everyone made their way to their assigned partners.

"Hey, stranger," Maya said, tossing her braids to the other side of her neck. "Is this seat taken?" Obviously it wasn't.

Maya sat down across from me. She smelled like peaches and fresh roses. Her green eyes matched the V-neck shirt she was wearing. I was so distracted I had forgotten what the assignment was. I felt my phone vibrate.

"Breathe." From Abbie.

"I'll go first. Don't forget to write down the major points, okay?" Maya looked me in the eyes, as if she was trying to search for something more.

"Yo tengo una tortuga. Su nombre es Sam. Tengo un hermano menor. Y me encanta jugar baloncesto."

Her eyes glistened when she spoke. Like every word that came pouring out of her was full of life. Maybe it was her speaking Spanish that took my breath away, but I'm betting it was just her.

"Okay, got all that? Your turn," Maya said, turning her notebook to a new page.

"Okay. Cool. Soy hijo único . . ."

Mrs. Dickens popped up from behind me, correcting me. "Almost, Gabriela. You mean hija única. Only daughter, not son."

The funny part was, whenever I spoke Spanish, I would always use the masculine noun. Why was that? It wasn't like I felt like a boy. Maybe I just knew more words that were masculine. Maybe I felt more attached with words that were masculine. I don't know. In the perfect situation it would just be neutral. Neutral faces and neutral responses made me question, but neutral language made me feel comfortable. And when I was the one speaking, I wanted to feel comfortable with what words came out of my mouth. I wanted to have control over that.

"Okay, no problem. Thanks, Señora," I said, slouching back into my chair.

Before I finished, Maya passed me a note. It was in Spanish.

It read: "Quieres salir conmigo?" Translation: Do you want to go out with me?

Before I could respond, she was writing down her phone number. She folded it up and put it in my hand. When I looked up, she was already sitting back at her seat across the room.

The rest of the class felt like a dream. Had the girl who was on my mind really just asked me out?

18

W hen I got home from school, I didn't even need to check to know that my mom was still in bed. I could feel the sadness pulling the air down in a dark and heavy way.

Everything was as I'd left it this morning, and Eliza and Cagney were nowhere in sight. There was an emptiness everywhere. I slowly tiptoed through the kitchen and cracked open my mom's bedroom door. Cagney was sleeping next to her head, and Eliza was curled next to her feet. Cats: the great protectors. I quietly slid into bed and wrapped my arms around my mom; she didn't wake up completely but softly squeezed my hand. This was home. Even if home wasn't always buzzing with joyful music.

I was worried that she hadn't eaten all day, so I slipped out of bed and went to the kitchen to warm up some soup for her and placed it on top of the dresser. A few hours later, I checked back in and saw the soup had been eaten.

The house was weeping with pain; my bones ached for my mom. I felt so helpless.

I finished my homework, straightened up a bit, put a load of laundry into the wash, and then took a shower as I waited for my laundry to dry. As I was folding my clothes, I felt something in the pocket of my pants. It was Maya's number. Mildly destroyed, but I tried my best to make out the numbers.

Now or never, Gabriela. Be fearless.

I typed in Maya's number in my phone and began to type her a message:

Sí, claro quiero salir contigo. (Yes, of course I want to go out with you). Yikes. Delete.

What do you mean when you say "go out"? You mean, like, as friends, or, like, go out go out? Like a date? Delete.

Hey. Delete forever.

Sup:) DELETE!!

{ 107 }

ME: Hey, it's gabriela. I squeezed my eyes shut and pressed Send.

I immediately saw text bubbles. She was typing! She was typing! Oh, my, god. She was typing.

> **MAYA:** i was hoping you'd text me
> **ME:** really?
> **MAYA:** yeah, of course. why else would i give you my number
> **ME:** i donno . . . why did you?
> **MAYA:** because I wanted you to have it

Wow, this conversation is going well. It's now or never. Just ask.

> **ME:** what did you mean when you asked me if i wanted to go out with you?
> **MAYA:** i meant, do you want to go out with me:)
> **ME:** but in what way?
> **MAYA:** i mean usually when people go out they leave their house and go somewhere else
> **ME:** lol, but do you mean like a date?
> **MAYA:** yes.

ME: i've never been on a date with a girl before. (*I'd never been on a date with anyone, actually.*)

MAYA: oh, sorry, i just thought, you were into girls. i saw your books you had, and well, to be honest, when we talk i sort of got that vibe.

ME: what vibe?

MAYA: the gay vibe

ME: oh . . .

MAYA: hey, it's not a bad thing. but it's totally cool if i read the vibe wrong

ME: you didn't read it wrong. *I can't believe I typed that.*

MAYA: good

ME: i mean, i don't know what i am, but i know that i want to go out with you. *Can't believe I typed that either.*

MAYA: works for me. let's just take it ~one day at a time~.

ME: did you just reference the show we're watching in Spanish?

MAYA: maybe? come at me?

ME: lol

MAYA: anyway, are you free this saturday? we could catch a movie downtown

ME: sure

MAYA: cool i'll see what's playing and get back to you

I threw my phone down like it was on fire and buried my face into my pillow. I couldn't believe it. I was finally going to go out with Maya. Everything felt perfect. Nothing could ruin this feeling.

Later that night, my heart was still chirping with excitement and then I started thinking about my mom again and I started to feel guilty for feeling so much joy. Why should I feel joy so easily and at this moment when my mom felt the way she did right now?

Though I still felt happy about Maya, I still felt sad about my mom. Could you be happy/sad?

As the sun began to set, I could feel my stomach screeching at me. I hadn't eaten in hours. I scrolled through videos on YouTube and found a new recipe.

I'd been cooking for myself since I was about nine. There were many days where I had to figure out what I was going to make to eat, so I took the opportunity to learn a lot of different cool meals. I was not going to be eating Kraft's mac and cheese every night—or, really, any night. No thanks—hard pass.

So I learned different recipes by watching nearly every episode on Tasty.

I would make enough for two so my mom could have the leftovers. Tonight, I was going to make breakfast for dinner. One of my mom's favorite meals. I scarfed down half, placed the rest in a Tupperware in the fridge, cleaned the kitchen, and headed to bed.

19

When Saturday came, my heart was ready to burst out of my chest. But the sweet songs of birds, the sun playfully hiding in between branches of trees, and the sound of Gloria Estefan's "Turn the Beat Around" calmed me down. I crawled out of bed and found my mom with cleaning gloves on and a bucket full of cleaning supplies at her disposal. Her back-and-forth motion across our wood table was going faster than the beat of the song.

This wasn't uncommon. When she crept out of her darkness, she'd often become extremely happy. In one of her workbooks she had, they described it as mania.

"Did you eat yet?" I asked, trying to find her above the music.

No reply. Instead, she grabbed me and started dancing with me as "Last Dance" by Donna Summer started playing. I danced. I smiled and laughed with her. I didn't want to signal anything was wrong in my facial expression and trigger her.

As we were dancing, my phone vibrated. It was Maya.

MAYA: let's meet at cineplex at 11:40.
ME: i'll be there.
ME: wait, what are we seeing?
MAYA: you'll see.
ME: okay . . .
MAYA: . . . don't . . . me!
ME: . . .
MAYA: lol see you soon

I turned down the radio and told my mom I was going to meet a friend. She barely stopped dancing, but kissed me and said to have fun. I wanted her to live in her version of joy, but I also wanted her to stop and look me in the eye and tell me that she was okay. Or say anything.

I flipped the volume back up as she continued to dance and slipped out the front door quietly.

Usually riding the train made me anxious. The noise, the smells, the fact that we were underground.

But today I was riding the train with confidence. What was waiting for me on the other side wasn't more noise or more unwanted smells. It was Maya.

When I got off the train, I turned on Google Maps. I had been to this movie theatre before, but normally my mom drove me. The last thing I wanted to do was get lost. As I neared the theatre, I spotted Maya. Even though she was surrounded by dozens of people, hers was the only face I noticed. She was carrying two huge tote bags. She looked down at her phone, then looked up and spotted me. I hoped she hadn't seen me drifting into space, watching her.

"Oh, good, you're here. Take one," she said playfully.

"What is this?" I asked.

"Oh, I didn't tell you? We're not going to the movies."

"What?"

"It's seventy-five degrees out. We aren't sitting in a dark room."

"Where are we going?" I asked.

"Is where we are going as important as where we are now?" She put her hand over mine. One touch from her made me forget. It made me forget how to formulate a sentence. It made me forget that my mom was home alone.

All of a sudden I felt guilty.

I pulled my hand away.

"Did I do something wrong?" Maya asked. Her voice sounded a little sunken and hurt.

"No, it's not that. I just . . ."

"Hey, it's okay. We don't have to hold hands. I won't touch you, deal?"

"I want you to hold my hand. But I don't know if I should be here."

Maya tried to follow along. "Where should you be?"

And that's when I spilled it. I told her everything. I told her all about my mom. I told her how she couldn't get out of bed in the morning. I told her how some days she would be super happy to the point of singing and cleaning all day. I told her that was probably what she was doing now.

Maya looked down at her phone, then gave it to me and said, "Put in your address, please!"

"What?"

"Just do it."

When we pulled up to my building in our Uber, I waved hello to Kassandra at the front desk and pushed 8 for our floor number.

As we approached the door we could hear music streaming out from the other side. My mom had gotten dressed but was still cleaning, her back to us. I went to the radio and turned down the music.

"Mom. Mom . . . Mom!"

"Yes, doll?" she answered without looking up from cleaning.

"This is Maya . . ."

Maya interrupted, "Hi, Mrs. Ricci. I'm a friend of Gabriela's. We brought some lunch."

Then whispered to me: "Lunch at the park would've beat the movies, right?"

I couldn't believe she had planned a picnic in the park. She was amazing. What was more amazing was that she'd sacrifice her plans to come back and check in on my mom with me.

"Oh honey, that's so sweet, I don't really have an appetite, why don't you two enjoy it," my mom said, barely looking up. She was doing anything outside of herself and her own emotions to stay distracted. I didn't want to put any more attention onto her, so I continued to act as if everything was okay.

Maya and I brought the two totes filled with our afternoon picnic to the terrace and began to eat.

"So," she said, opening up some mac and cheese, which was a huge step up from Kraft's, that's for sure. She took out a piece of cornbread and split it with me. "This isn't exactly where we were going for our first date."

"Is where we were going as important as where we are now?" I said, smiling at her and popping a few grapes into my mouth.

20

Twenty-four hours ago, I wasn't sure who I was or where I belonged. Twenty-four hours ago, I felt invisible. Twenty-four hours ago, I had no idea who I was. I still was not completely sure, but I felt now like I was getting there. If Dinah Washington had the optimism of how twenty-four little hours could change a circumstance, I was hopeful I could, too.

I spent the rest of the night finishing *Annie on My Mind* and texting Maya. I wasn't sure what was next for us. All I knew was that nothing could stop the dizzy funny feeling I felt.

But when I got out of the shower I came back to frantic texts and missed calls from Héctor.

HÉCTOR: my brother just got jumped.

I called him back, and before I could ask what happened, he started telling me. His speaking was painful, and it was hard for me to hear every word between every gasp, and him struggling to hold back tears.

"It's Arturo. They jumped him. They messed him up real bad. Can you meet me at the hospital? Please, I need a friend." Héctor's voice was cracking.

"I'm on my way."

My mom was still in so much of a manic state, even though I told her where I was going, she didn't really acknowledge it. Instead, I ordered an Uber under her account. I wanted to be there for my new friend.

When I got to the hospital, I introduced myself to Héctor's parents and David, Arturo's boyfriend. I hugged Héctor and asked how Arturo was doing.

"They said he'll be fine. A few broken ribs and a broken arm."

"That's so horrible," I said, holding back tears.

"This isn't the first time," Héctor replied, barely making eye contact. "Before we moved here he was jumped by some kids at school. He didn't want to press charges. And guess what, he doesn't want to press charges—again! He can be so thick headed. He wants to believe people are good. What good person knocks someone out so hard that they are unconscious?" He was stammering.

David interjected, "I feel like it was my fault. I was inside trying to find my coat because I was stupid enough to leave it in the first place. I should have been there."

"Where did it happen? Are you sure you can't convince your Arturo to press charges?" I asked David.

"We were at Blue Velvet. A gay club downtown. We always go. There's only so many safe spaces we have as LGBTQIA+ people." David threw his jacket onto a chair. "Now I never want to step foot inside again."

My mind quickly started thinking about Maya and me. What if we had gone to the park yesterday and someone saw us holding hands? Would they try to hurt us too? Why would who I like bother people we don't even know? The thought angered me. But, mostly, it scared me. I didn't want to be afraid to be me.

I stayed at the hospital for a couple hours until I realized it was getting late. I usually didn't take an

Uber this far into the night. I wasn't sure how I was going to get home—I knew I couldn't call Mom.

"I should get going," I said, looking at my phone with the Uber app open.

Before I said another word, David offered to drive me home.

We sat in silence in his busted Toyota Camry and listened to a remix of Kacey Musgraves's "High Horse" as he drove me through Brooklyn.

"Who remixed this?" I asked.

"Hmm. Good question. I'm trying to get more into it. But I love the original."

We sat in silence again.

Silence never bothered me. I was used to all kinds of silence with my mom. But this was a fed-up and angry type of silence. Words unspoken still had a way of breathing fire.

"What a way to end the weekend," David finally tried to joke, to break the quiet.

I asked softly, "Does this kind of thing happen a lot?" I was hesitant to ask such a direct question, for fear of knowing the truth and for fear of sounding ignorant.

"People fear what they don't understand. Our existence angers people because we challenge the norm. But I'm not going to stop being me because it makes people more comfortable. I love Arturo, and that's all that matters," David finished, holding back tears.

The car stopped, and he asked if I wanted him to walk me in. I told him I was good and quickly walked into my building.

Just as I had started to feel happy for being me, the thought that kept creeping up in the back of my mind was that not everyone was going to be happy for me being me. And people wanted to hurt people like me.

I didn't want to be afraid.

When I got back home, my mom was already asleep and I couldn't sleep. I decided to go back to my English essay. I went to the folded pages, ripped them out, and threw them into the trash to start fresh. I spent all of Sunday revising my essay.

21

When I got to English on Monday, Mrs. Andersen was writing THE AGENDA on the board. Instead of getting together with our critique partner this time, she gave us a prompt, saying it may help us with our essay and allow us to dig deeper.

> PROMPT: Where do you feel the most at home? How has community made you feel at home?

I bit the end of my pen, repeating the prompt in my head over and over. It was hard to use any of the self-soothing skills or coping skills my mom tried at home during class. I stuck to fidgeting and trying to accept my thoughts. And remembering moments of joy.

I felt joy at home with my mom. With my cats. With music. There was nothing that stopped me from feeling at home, even when my mom was deeply depressed, because I accepted that piece of her. I'd felt scared and unsafe, but never at home. But there were people who made me feel like I didn't belong in other spaces that felt like home to me.

As I looked around the classroom, I was reminded how everyone in my life was white. My mom, my family, our extended family and friends. I also always seemed to have white friends. At school there'd always been this invisible separation between white kids and kids of color. Two cultures. Two separate sets of rules—rules I never felt I had access to. I never really fit in with the kids of color. I didn't speak Spanish fluently; I didn't share their same culture. I didn't even dress the same. I felt like I was a stranger in my own home. I felt like I was my own home, my own race. How had community made me feel at home? I was still figuring that one out.

If I could write *adopted* every time a form at a doctor's office asked, I would. I'd always watch my mom proudly check *Hispanic* for me, but I felt like I was an imposter. What made me more Hispanic than white? What makes someone their race? If it was culture, food, language, and traditions, then I definitely was not Hispanic. So, I tried to stay in my lane and stick to what I knew—which was "being" white, which to me felt more like home than anything else I'd ever known.

I think, maybe, I mostly stopped myself from feeling like home among other Hispanic people. But I'd tried to befriend a couple other Hispanic people before, and they wanted nothing to do with me. One time, a girl in my class laughed at me, saying I was nothing like her and would never be like her. Maybe she was right, but I hadn't gotten to choose my family any more than she had. Ever since that experience I never put myself out there again. I didn't know if I could ever feel at home with anyone other than what I already knew.

"Pencils down!" Mrs. Andersen's voice chimed.

Even though I may not put any of this in my essay, it felt really good to get it out.

Words.

I felt at home with words.

22

I was a few minutes late for Spanish because I had stayed after to talk to Mrs. Andersen a little more. When I got to Spanish, Abbie had saved me a seat. Normally I sat in the front row at the desk nearest to the window, but no one had ever saved me a seat so I didn't want to turn down this possible once-in-a-lifetime opportunity.

"Sorry I'm a little late. I thought I lost my glasses, but they were on my head the entire time," Mrs. Dickens said, shuffling in with her usual four bags over her shoulders. She always looked like she was coming back from a weekend trip.

Abbie rushed over to help her unload.

"Buenas tardes, clase, y gracias, Abbie," she said as her glasses fell down her nose. "I'm going to be passing out journals. Each day I want you to log how many times you use Spanish in your daily lives. It could be at the grocery store, or ordering breakfast. Our community is filled with Spanish speakers. Oh and any Spanish spoken in class or at home won't count," she added, peering at me. It was funny how everyone assumed I spoke Spanish just because of what I looked like.

"You can choose to do this alone or work with classmates. I want to see you using Spanish at least once a day, though. Be sure to include the date, time, and setting you used Spanish. By the end of the month everyone should have at least logged thirty times. Oh, and one more thing. The person you speak Spanish with must be able to answer you in Spanish."

Abbie nudged me. "Your parents speak Spanish, right?"

"No, they don't." I didn't know why I said *they*. I could explain later.

"A lot of people don't speak their first language in their homes anymore. My mom told me that when she was a kid, she would spend all her time trying to lose her accent."

"Why would she want to do that?" I said, organizing my pens.

"Sometimes people are afraid of being different. They don't want to be treated differently. Maybe that's why I am the way I am. I don't want to hide or feel I have to change to make others more comfortable."

Before I could process what Abbie was saying, she was waving me over closer and talking a mile a minute.

"My mom isn't home from Cambodia yet, but my abuelita lives with us, and my dad is actually pretty awesome. You want to come over for dinner? If Abuelita is feeling up to it, I'm sure she could whip us up some ceviche. Have you ever had ceviche? We could plan out the spots we could hit up to speak Spanish. My vote is going to the Bronx."

"I would love to. I just have to ask my mom."

"Just text her now, and then come home with me after school!" Abbie said, smiling.

I took out my phone quickly, and I told my mom I was going over to Abbie's house for dinner. As class was ending, I got her text back.

"Okay, sweetie."

Chairs screeched from under desks, and feet pounded on the ground toward the exit when the bell rang. I thoughtfully put my books away, and Abbie said she'd meet me outside.

When I got outside, I closed my eyes. I felt the cool breeze on my skin, and quickly my daydream washed over my mind. Before I could get to the end of the dream, I was interrupted by the sound of yelling. This time it wasn't Jonathan making snide remarks, but his friend, Matt. Jonathan's face, behind him, was bright red like a tomato.

"It's a simple question, freak. Were you born a girl or boy? What are you hiding under there?" Matt taunted, trying to pull Abbie's hair.

I rushed over. I wasn't sure what I was going to do or say, but I knew I had to be there for my friend. Before anything else happened, Mrs. Andersen was in the middle of Matt and Abbie.

"Break it up right now. Matt. See me in the Principal's office NOW."

"But the bell's gonna ring any second!" Matt groaned.

"I don't care . . . This is NOT how we treat people," Mrs. Andersen shouted.

Matt shuffled behind Mrs. Andersen, and Abbie frantically fixed her hair, patting dirt off her backpack and walking toward me as if nothing had happened.

"Are you okay?" I said, consoling her.

"Oh, that?" she replied, trying to brush it off. "That's nothing."

As we waited for the light to change, a voice called out from behind us.

"Hey!"

I turned around to see Jonathan, his hand nervously in his hair.

He continued: "That was really messed up for Matt to do. I promise I had no idea he was going to do that. That's not me. That's him."

Was this his idea of an apology?

"I'm really sorry that happened," Jonathan went on. "I know I'm not the nicest to any of you, but that was way messed up. Anyway, yeah, I gotta go." He turned the corner before either of us could respond.

My mom has always taught me to see the good in people and that hurt people hurt people. I guess this counted as some good. But I couldn't understand why someone would willingly hang out with people who were that much crueler than him. Not that Jonathan had been that much more amazing up till now. I focused my attention back to Abbie.

"Abbie," I said cautiously, "what do you mean that was nothing? Are you saying that happens a lot to you?"

"I mean, being me isn't always a day at the park. Even if I act like it is." I noticed the same flash of emptiness in her eyes that I'd seen in my mom. But she quickly adjusted her shirt and held her head up high. She had the same sense of humor as David. Pushing down the real emotion and covering it up with a joke.

We walked in silence until we reached her house.

The first step into Abbie's home was like walking on set of a cooking show. The smell of cilantro, lime, and onions filled the air. It was incredible. Abbie hung her bag on a hook, and I followed her lead.

"Abuelita, soy yo!" Abbie yelled, walking toward the kitchen.

Abbie's grandma was listening to upbeat Latin music while blissfully juicing limes.

"Abuelita, this is my friend, Gabriela." Abbie's grandma wiped her hands on her apron and kissed me on both cheeks, smiling hello with her eyes.

"My grandma doesn't speak that much English. But that's her way of greeting you. Besides, she thinks people speak best through food and music."

"Then I guess we just had a conversation," I said, smiling at her.

"Exactly!" Abbie laughed, reaching into the rice cooker to steal a taste. Her abuelita swatted her hand away playfully. I started imagining what it would be like to have an abuelita to come home to, one who played Latin music and cooked authentic Latino food. I never knew my grandparents either. It's always been my mom and me.

I decided to try to use the little Spanish I knew to ask her who the singer was. I knew I wouldn't get to count this for my journal, but I didn't care.

"¿Qué cantante es esto?" I tried, stumbling on my words, knowing my accent probably sounded garbled and weird.

Even though we both could tell my Spanish wasn't perfect, Abbie's abuelita answered as if I'd spoken the best Spanish she ever heard.

"El se llama Antonio Cartagena," she said, walking over to the radio and turning it up.

Even though I didn't grow up listening to Latin music, I had always been drawn to it. I was also intimidated by it, and it took me to a place of uncertainty that I was never ready to fully explore.

Abuelita asked Abbie something, and she turned to me.

"My grandma asked if you speak Spanish. I told her not fluently. You were saying that your parents don't speak Spanish. Why don't they?" She started scarfing down her ceviche.

"Well, the truth is it's my mom who doesn't speak Spanish. And, uh, I don't know my dad. I don't have one because my mom never got married, and she doesn't speak Spanish because she's Italian. I . . . I was adopted." As I finished I started stuffing my face with rice too, so I could have time to think of an answer to any follow-up questions.

"Ah! That makes sense. That's cool. You want to try some chicha morada?" Abbie asked, wiping her mouth with the back of her hand. I was surprised she didn't have a million questions like most people but relieved I didn't have to explain myself. How do you explain why you were adopted anyway? I just was.

"Definitely," I said, taking a huge gulp, not even knowing what it was.

"Not bad, right?" Abbie asked, smiling at her abuelita.

"It's delicious. What's in it?"

"Ask my abuelita," she said, gleaming.

"¿Qué tiene en la chicha morada?" I asked, pretty sure most of it was understandable.

"Tiene maíz morado, manzana, y piña."

"¡Qué delicioso!" I replied as Abuelita poured me another glass. I whispered to Abbie, asking what she had said.

"It's purple corn, apple, and pineapple. Maybe one day you can come over and help her prepare it. She'd love that."

By the time we finished eating and helping clean up, Abbie's dad walked in and made his way to the refrigerator. Abuelita had saved him a serving.

I was expecting Abbie's dad to be Latino too, but I wasn't sure what he was.

"Trying to guess what my dad's ethnicity is?" Abbie smiled, interrupting my thought bubble.

"Is he Latino too?" I said.

"Nope. He's Indian. My mom's Peruvian." Abbie plopped herself onto the couch and flicked through the TV channels. "Now stop creeping on my dad, and let's go upstairs!"

"So does that mean you also speak Hindi?"

"First, thanks for not saying *Hindu*. Second, I barely speak Spanish. If I was fluent, would I really be in your class?"

"True," I said, laughing.

Abbie turned off the TV and snuck up behind her dad, who was eating his leftovers, and gave him a hug.

"Daddy, this is my new friend, Gabriela. We are in Spanish class together. We're working on a project together too. Which we are totally going to get an A on," she said, batting her eyelashes.

"Nice to meet you, Gabriela. I'm Mr. Mehta." He reached out his hand to shake mine.

"Hi. It's nice to meet you." I said stiffly, reaching for his hand. Mr. Mehta smiled.

"Okay! So you've met. Come on, Gabriela, let's go study." Abbie grabbed my hand and led me down the hall to her room.

Abbie's room was awesome. Her bed was like a bunk bed, except for the fact that there wasn't a bed underneath. Instead of a second bed she had a hammock, beanbag chair, a record player, huge speakers, and a collection of vinyl records in huge crates. Abbie threw off some of the clothes on her beanbag and sank right in.

"So what do you want to do? Want to figure out where we are going tomorrow? I still vote the Bronx."

"I honestly don't think my mom would let me go that far," I said.

"True, it's really far. Let's just go to some bodegas around here," Abbie replied.

"Deal."

◎ ◎ ◎

"I'm so happy you're finding community," my mom said to me one morning as she made her coffee.

I looked up from my bowl of cereal. "Yeah . . . Yeah. I am, too."

My mom slide into the chair next to me. "Why do you not seem happy about that?"

I placed my spoon on top of my cereal. "Oh, oops, that's not how I meant for it to come out. I guess, I'm just feeling almost in awe of it. In awe that I could finally, possibly, maybe, have friends . . . have community. So, when you said it that way, it was so beautifully put and so beautifully said. Thanks, Mom."

"For?"

"For being you."

"I'm just happy to see my baby happy. I know that I can't be everything for you and I wouldn't want to be. No offense . . ." She knocked her knee with mine.

"None taken, but do go on." I smirked.

"Well, I said what I said. I love my kid and I will support anyone who makes them feel valued and loves them for exactly who they are."

"This feels like a very cinematic moment. Don't get a tear drop in your coffee."

"Mmhmmm," my mom said, raising an eyebrow, and taking a big gulp of coffee.

◎ ◎ ◎

For the next few weeks Abbie and I were inseparable. It was nice to have somewhere to go when I knew my mom wasn't going through another depressive episode because I knew she was doing her thing by herself and was okay.

We worked on our Spanish homework, and we even helped each other finish our English assignment.

"Do you know what you're going to do for the 'other piece' of your English assignment?" I asked one day, sprawled upside down on her beanbag.

"Well, a YouTube video would be so obvious. Everyone stans a creator, but I don't want to be predictable. Predictable? I don't know her. What about you?"

I let out a huge sigh. "I'm big worried because I don't really think I'm actually good at anything. I thought I was good at writing, but when Héctor saw a draft the first time, he had so much to say."

"Just because he had an opinion doesn't mean he didn't like it. It also doesn't mean you're not a good writer. You're way too hard on yourself, Gabriela."

"Mood," I said, biting my inner cheek.

"Big mood. Hey, why don't *you* just do a YouTube video? I can teach you the ropes? Why am I asking? We're doing this!"

"Oh my god—I—"

"So, that's a yes!" Abbie then pretended to use the top of her hand as a microphone and patted down on it to see if the "microphone" was on.

"Is this thing on? Test, testing, one, two, three. It's Abbie, reporting live. And it appears to be iconic."

We both started cracking up.

I actually felt myself getting excited about the project again. Although, to be completely honest, it usually didn't take much to make me excited about school, unless I felt like I wasn't good at something. I don't know where I got that insecurity from. My mom definitely didn't teach me that.

Between spending time with her abuelita, cooking and speaking Spanish with her, and getting closer to Abbie, it felt a little like a piece of me that had been missing was starting to feel whole.

Abbie's dad saw we were spending so much time together that he even invited my mom over for dinner. I was happy he did because I didn't want my mom to think I was replacing her.

"Thank you for inviting me to dinner, Mr. Mehta," my mom said that night, with a slight glee to her voice when we walked in.

"Please, don't thank me. It is my pleasure—and, maybe honestly, selfish on my part too. I have never seen Abbie so happy."

"Dad, I'm right here. Literally. I heard that."

"Good. I'm happy you heard that. Literally."

Abbie and I grinned at each other.

"Abuelita, do you know that Gabriela is more fluent in Spanish now because of you?"

"Ah? Really?" Abuelita replied in English.

"Really!" Abbie and I said in unison.

". . . more or less," I added. We all laughed.

I watched my mom eating in silence that night. I studied her. Maybe more than I should. Maybe more than what made her comfortable. I wanted to make sure she was okay. All the time. I felt a sensation in my chest squeeze me from the insides.

My mom turned her head to me about halfway through the dinner and smiled. It was a smile I hadn't really seen before.

23

Finally, we passed in our Spanish-conversation logs. Abbie and I had explored nearly every bodega in Brooklyn and even went to the Lower East Side and all the way up to Washington Heights. We talked to people in barber shops, waitresses, cooks, and went into the Spanish section of bookstores to speak to people in Spanish. I was so excited to show my mom all of our hard work after it was graded.

But when I got home from school that day, no music filled the air. I looked into my mom's room; she wasn't there. I looked on the radio for a note. Nothing. I went to the terrace; she wasn't there. I opened the door to the bathroom, hoping to find my mom trying to decide between earrings. She wasn't there either.

As I walked to her room to look for her again, I saw her legs poking out from the side of the bed. My cats were licking her feet and surrounding her. I shooed them away. My hands were shaking. I quickly looked around her room. There was a bottle of sleeping pills that was open, but there weren't any pills on the ground, and there were still enough for at least half a month. I knew my mom wouldn't purposefully do something. I knew it.

I knew it.

I didn't know if I knew it.

I needed to believe it.

I quickly reached for my phone to call 9-1-1. My mom told me to always call 9-1-1 if an adult wasn't there and if it was a medical emergency. I thought I would have been prepared to make this call. But who could prepare for a call like this? I was shaking so much that my fingers just barely pressed the right numbers.

My cats came huddling near me. I could feel that they were as tense and worried as I was. I connected to the operator and told her my mom wasn't moving but she was breathing and told them my address.

Before the room began to spin, I quickly texted Abbie to tell her I needed her and her dad to meet me at Mt. Sinai. I told her I was okay but that my mom had passed out.

When I came to, I found myself in a hospital bed.

"What happened?" I asked drowsily.

"You passed out, honey," a nurse answered, motioning someone to come over.

"Why? Where am I? Where's my mom? Is she okay?"

Before she responded, a tall brown man with Coke-bottle glasses came over to me and introduced himself as Dr. Singh.

"Hi, Gabriela. My name is Dr. Singh. You've gone through quite an ordeal. I want you to know that your mother is okay. We've evaluated her, and she's going to be going to an in-patient facility. Do you know what that is?"

"Yes." I knew what it was because she had gone there before.

Dr. Singh continued: "You found your mom, and you did the right thing by calling nine-one-one. We want to make sure you have the proper living arrangements while she is getting better. Your mom listed your aunt as her emergency contact."

"Okay—but what happened to her?"

"Your mom ingested too much of her sleeping medication."

"You mean she overdosed?" I said angrily. "You can say it, I'm not a child." He was treating me like I couldn't handle the truth.

"Yes. That's correct."

"Okay. Thanks for telling me . . . Uh, my aunt lives on Long Island."

"I just got off the phone with her. And your aunt talked to Mr. Mehta, who I understand is your best friend's dad?"

Best friend. I had never heard anyone say it out loud. I guess she was.

"Yeah, she's my best friend," I said, still groggy and annoyed with the doctor.

"Your aunt and Mr. Mehta spoke, and he's happy to have you stay with them while your mom is a patient here. Your aunt will fax over all the paperwork to sign off on that legally, and your mom is also signing off on that arrangement. How does that all sound?"

"Okay . . . great . . . weird, but cool," I said, trying to sit up. "I want to talk to my mom first. Please!"

"She's resting right now. Soon, don't you fret." Dr. Singh motioned to his nurse and looked back at me. "Let's keep her hydrated."

Her.

I may have been out of it, but I and my body still had a reaction.

"You have some visitors. Would you like to see them?"

"Okay." *Okay* was all I could get myself to say further.

As I tried to drink the juice the nurse had brought to me, I saw three figures walking toward me. It was Héctor, Abbie, and Maya. Abbie must have sent a group chat to everyone.

"We heard about what happened. I'm so sorry, Gabriela. On the bright side, you get to stay with me," Abbie said.

Héctor elbowed Abbie and glared at her. "If you need anything—anything at all—let me know. You were there for my brother, and I want to be there for you and your mother," he added.

"Thanks. That means a lot," I said, clearing my throat.

"We're gonna hit up the cafeteria. Do you want anything?" Héctor signaled Abbie to come with him.

"Nah, I'm good. Thanks."

When Héctor and Abbie left, Maya walked up to my bed with her hands behind her back. "Pick a hand."

I reached out to tap her left hand.

She pulled her hand from behind her back and had a bag of grapes. I smiled.

"Our one and only date is symbolized by grapes," I said weakly.

"Well, don't you want to know what's in my other hand?" she asked with a singing smile.

"Of course I do."

"Close your eyes first."

I closed my eyes.

"Okay, now look."

When I looked down I saw *Jeff Buckley: Live at Sin-é* sitting on my lap.

"How did you know I love Jeff?" I felt my eyes tearing up with happiness.

"Let's say I did a little research on you," she replied as she gently grabbed my hand.

"Héctor?" I asked, my hand melting into her hand.

"Okay, so Héctor may have helped. He does have access to everything you've ever bought at his store." She squeezed my hand.

Maya reached into her bag and pulled out a CD player. "I know, these things are ancient. I found it in my dad's room. But I want you to listen to your CD and relax. Can you do that for me?" She opened up the CD and put it into the player and placed the headphones on me.

I spent a couple of days in the hospital and talked to my mom only one time over the phone. Dr. Singh checked in on me and kept reassuring me that she was okay. I even had time to rewrite my English essay (*again*) and think more about what I would say in my video. But now, the only thing on my mind was my mom.

I should have been there.

24

I'm sure that in less sad circumstances staying with Abbie would have been so much fun. Instead, I felt like I was embarrassingly sad and always in the way. And even still, Abbie and her family were overly accommodating and understanding each time I passed up dinner, or a snack, or watching TV.

When I got back to school, I passed in my essay to Mrs. Andersen. Before I even got to my seat and the rest of the class trickled in, Mrs. Andersen had written me a note to see the school counselor.

"I'm here to support you. We all are. Come back to class when you're ready," she said with sorrowful eyes.

Mr. Shapiro had long black hair that he wrapped up in a bun, revealing an undercut. His skin was covered in tattoos like a beautiful mural. He had the kind of tattoos celebrities or people who were tattoo artists have.

At the edge of his desk there was a wedding photo. The two people in the photo were at the edge of the ocean, holding each other as the sunset kissed the sky. They even had their small dog in the photo too. It was truly the definition of picture perfect.

He began by asking if I knew why I was there.

I shoved my hands into my pocket and stared at the ground, not answering.

"Gabriela, I'm terribly sorry to hear about your mom. Mental illness doesn't only affect the individual, it affects the whole family. You have my support."

How did you know all that? I asked with my eyes.

"Your mom called the school because she thought it would be best if you had someone in school to talk to. I'd say you have a pretty phenomenal mom."

"Yeah, I know. And I talked to her a few times already. Short calls. Like, I could hear someone in the background telling her time was almost up. But I heard her voice, so that's something . . . right?" I asked with my arms crossed and a straight face.

"I'm happy you were able to talk to her. How did that feel?" Mr. Shapiro asked.

"It was okay, I guess."

"I see." Mr. Shapiro paused for a moment. "How are you feeling right now, Gabriela?"

Where did I even start? Instead of talking about my mom, I directed the conversation back to my essay. "I'm feeling confused," I muttered.

He must have been used to muttering pre-teens and replied instantly, "What are you confused about?"

"I don't know who I am. The project we are working on is all about that. How am I supposed to know?"

"Hmm. Very insightful. I want to be transparent with you and tell you that I spoke to each of your teachers individually, Gabriela, because I want everyone to be on the same page and be of support to you. I was just talking to Mrs. Andersen this morning about your big English project, and what I've gathered is that the project isn't about knowing who you are, but about telling your story. However raw or confusing it may be. Living as your true self doesn't mean knowing all the answers. It means being okay with the unknown and embracing who you are in this very moment."

I couldn't help staring at his wedding photo. It was as if I was desperately trying to memorize it in an attempt to transfer that picture perfect happiness onto myself.

As I continued to stare at the photo, I also couldn't help but notice that Mr. Shapiro looked different in the photo. His shoulders were less broad and his hips weren't as slim; his face was also a bit clearer. A little softer and more youthful.

I could hear his voice, but I felt like I had left my body and was watching our conversation in his hipster-man-den of an office.

"Were you living your authentic self? Were you happy in this picture?" I blurted out, pointing to the wedding photo.

"If we're being honest, my answer is yes and no. Yes, I was on the road to living my authentic self." He reached into his pocket and pulled out his phone, to an album labeled *Pre-T*.

"In this photo, I had just started wearing binders. It was the first time I began to see myself."

"What's Pre-T, and what's a binder?"

"*Pre-T* means before I started taking hormone replacement therapy. The hormone is called testosterone. Testosterone is the main hormone that helps female to male, or FTM, people achieve the common traits that males have. That's where the letter *T* comes from in Pre-T. Binders are meant to help give the appearance of a flatter chest. Many transgender men and non-binary people wear them. It makes them more comfortable in their skin. More authentic to who they are."

There was that word again. *Authentic.*

"Mr. Shapiro . . . I had no idea you were transgender. Are you saying you were born a girl or a boy?"

"I was assigned female at birth, AFAB for short. But I always knew I was male. I'm a trans man. And those assigned male at birth that don't feel they—"

"Don't feel they identify with their gender assigned at birth," I said cutting him off, accidentally. I remembered that from YouTube videos I watched.

"Exactly! If that person felt that way, they may identify as being a trans woman. But it's a little more complicated than that. Gender lives on a spectrum. Everyone feels differently about their gender. So, the best thing to do is to respect peoples' identities and use the pronouns they ask you to use. But back to your question . . . was I happy? I was learning to be happy. I was learning to accept who I was."

I listened to Mr. Shapiro as he talked. So many of these words were new to me. I wanted to learn more. I wanted to understand.

"May I ask you a question now? Since you've flipped the tables on me." He said this with a grin.

"Yeah?" I replied, still going over everything he said in my head.

"How do you identify, and what are your pronouns?"

Why did everyone keep asking me this?

I thought for a minute, then answered.

"I've never really felt completely comfortable in my body. I'm not sure what it means. But I know that wearing anything girls would wear makes me uncomfortable."

"I see. So when you say 'what girls would wear,' what does that mean to you?"

"Well, you know. Anything in the girls' section. I don't shop in the girls' section. I never have."

"Ah, I see. When we talk about clothing, we begin to talk about how society has grouped this concept of male and female identities. Clothes are a way to one: not be naked and two: express to the world who we are. Clothing has a remarkable way of reveal-ing or sometimes concealing who we are. But it's important to know that clothing doesn't have a gen-der! How can fabric have a gender?"

"I guess I never thought about it that way," I said, glancing at the ceiling.

"Isn't it liberating to know?" Mr. Shapiro responded merrily.

"Yeah, a little bit. Maybe a lot," I answered. I could feel my heart starting to beat at a steadier rate.

"Tell me, have you ever heard of the terms *gender nonconforming* or *non-binary*?"

I shoved my hands in my hoodie pocket, my fin-gers searching for gum in the dark.

I popped a piece of gum into my mouth and chewed nervously. "No."

"Do you ever watch YouTube?"

"Yeah . . ." I tried not to laugh at his wording. *Watch YouTube.*

"Let me throw you some links." He started rip-ping out a piece of paper from his notebook.

"Okay." *Okay* was the only word that could come out of my mouth. Even though I was feeling more than the word *okay*. I was feeling relieved, excited, seen, with a dash of confusion. Could I fit into one of those definitions? Was this dark void inside of me going to be filled?

"Okay is totally valid. Thank you for sharing today, Gabriela. I enjoyed learning about you. And I thiiiiink ... that's all the time that we have for today." Mr. Shapiro paused and pointed up as the bell rings. "Pretty good, right?" He continued, "I look forward to talking more."

"Thanks, Mr. Shapiro." I said, smiling without my teeth and leaving for lunch.

As I shoved the list of YouTube videos to watch into my pocket, I turned the corner to the cafeteria and saw Jonathan and his dad in the hall. His dad was towering over him and shouting at him. A few oblivious teachers had even closed their doors because of the noise.

The only reason why I knew his dad was because he used to be the loudest parent in the stands during baseball games. He was asked to leave so many times that he was banned from coming to any more games. When I was younger, Jonathan and I were kinda friendly to each other. I guess when you got to middle school, everyone forgot about elementary friendships.

Jonathan watched his dad storm away and then snapped at me, "What are you staring at, freak? Are you bananas like your mom too?"

I guess he had forgotten about saying sorry to me. I was too tired to even have anything to say back to him.

"Are you okay?" I asked, approaching him.

"Don't worry about it," Jonathan said, wiping his tears and turning away. His face was red with humiliation.

I don't know what came over me. Whether it was Mr. Shapiro, thinking about how amazing my friends were, or what. But I walked toward him, toward one of the meanest people I knew, and reached my arms out to hug him. I kept thinking about how a hug or act of affection was what he really deserved. He didn't pull away.

"If you want, you should sit with me and my friends at lunch." Still hugging him.

"Why?" he said, pulling up his jeans and releasing himself from my embrace.

"What do you mean 'why'?" I asked.

"I treat you like trash," he said. "Why would you want anything to do with me?" He was using his sleeve as a tissue now.

"I mean, true!" I replied, making him laugh. "But that doesn't mean that can't change. People can change."

"Not everyone, Gabriela." He said my name for the first time in years.

"I think you can." Even though I knew he was talking about his dad, not about himself.

"You really are a weirdo, aren't you?" This time, he was joking around. I smiled at him.

"I will take that as my first compliment from you!"

When I got to the cafeteria, Maya, Héctor, and Abbie were in mid-laughter. Their eyes lit up when I approached the table.

"How are you!" Maya grabbed my hands, pulled me in closer, and whispered: "I missed you."

"Gabster! You're back!" Héctor exclaimed.

"Well, you're staying with me and we walked to school together, so, like, I know you're back," Abbie said.

I shook my head. "True, but you haven't seen me since eight fifteen this morning. Obviously the distance between us was heartbreaking."

"Gabs got jokes." Héctor smiled, playing with his food.

Since my mom was in rehab, she obviously couldn't pack me lunch, so I would be buying lunch. Today was meatloaf. That was a hard pass. I made my way to the salad bar and saw Jonathan from the corner of my eye.

"What are you looking at?" he said.

"The invitation is still open," I answered as I grabbed my salad and walked back to my table.

As I was mid-sentence with my friends, talking about how cool Mr. Shapiro was, Jonathan walked over.

I smiled, and he sat down.

Abbie side-eyed me and let out a small warm smile.

"So, how about that essay project for English?" I said.

Everyone groaned.

"Dude. Two rules at lunch. No politics or talking about school," Héctor said laughing.

Jonathan laughed too.

"Any idea what you're going to do for your second part of the English project?" Héctor asked Jonathan.

"Ha. I don't even know what I'm going to do with the first part," Jonathan said, sounding embarrassed.

"Hey, if you ever need any help, Gabriela's the writer, I'm the creator, and Héctor is our sound and music producer," Abbie exclaimed.

"Oh my gosh, since . . . when?" I asked.

"Since always. I just said it out loud just now though," Abbie said, smiling.

"Dang. I would really like that. Thanks, guys," Jonathan said, looking surprised.

"Ya'll," Héctor corrected Jonathan.

"What's the difference?"

"*Ya'll* includes everyone. *Ya'll* really means you all. People always assume people are cis or straight or the dominant culture. *Ya'll* is inclusive."

"Heard. I get it. Sorry ya'll."

25

Abbie and I both had a free period at the end of the day, so we decided to ditch and go back to her house early. She wanted me to help her with a YouTube video she was putting up soon. I didn't know how I could help.

Being on camera wasn't my thing. I avoided selfies at all costs, and I never knew where to look when FaceTiming. I was horrible at public speaking; I was barely going to be able to make a video for my own project. But Abbie insisted she needed my help. And I would help her in any way I could.

"Okay, so I was thinking about doing a series where I invite my queer friends to speak about their own experiences." Abbie was talking in between chugs of the strawberry milk she had made for us. "I know that in order to get a wider fanbase, I need to broaden my topics. What do you think?"

"That's an awesome idea," I said.

"True. It is pretty awesome. So, do you want to be the first guest?" She wiped her mouth with her sleeve as she poured more strawberry syrup into her cup.

"Abbie, I don't think I'm ready. Plus, I don't even know if I'm queer. I wouldn't even know what to say. Have you asked Héctor?"

She smiled. "I understand. I'm gonna ask Héctor. But know that you were the first person I asked."

"I'm honored," I said, as we clinked our strawberry milks together.

26

Before I knew it, Abbie had texted Héctor and he was over within twenty minutes, skateboard in hand and out of breath.

"I heard there was a casting call for incredibly handsome queer people. I'd like to audition," Héctor announced.

"You've come to the right place!" Abbie replied happily, looking him over with her lensless glasses.

"I had this idea that we could all—when every-one's ready"— Abbie glanced at me—"have our own segments and share our own stories." She explained the series to Héctor.

"I think that's such a cool idea!" Héctor said, rolling his skateboard back and forth with his feet.

"You think Maya would want to be part of this too, Gabriela?" Abbie asked.

"Maybe? I'll ask her."

"By the way, dude, you never told us how this Maya thing started. Can I just say one little itsy-bitsy thing . . . ?" Before I could reply Héctor said with a devilish smile: "I *knew* you were into her."

I could feel my face turning red.

"Yeah, you were right." I put my hand into my hoodie pocket. "I was actually shocked. I mean, we were in Spanish class, and she asked me out in Spanish."

"It's true. I literally saw it all happen," Abbie chimed in.

"Oh my god, you heard it?" I asked, embarrassed.

"Well, yeah. I was *right* behind you." She smiled and guzzled the last sip of strawberry milk.

"Wow, in Spanish?" Héctor breathed dreamily. "That's hecka romantic."

"Yeah, it was super cute. So, yeah. We're hanging out. I don't really know what we are. I don't really want to label it."

"Word," Héctor, a man of many words, said.

"Hey, we just like to see you happy, Gabriela. No one's asking you to label it. You don't even have to label yourself. Sorry for asking you to be a guest on my show. I shouldn't have made you feel like I was pushing you to label yourself or tell your story." Abbie was looking down now at her curled toes in her pink fuzzy socks.

"Don't worry about it. I'm just not sure about much. But I know that I like Maya and she likes me." I cleared my throat and continued, "But can I ask ya'll something?"

"Of course you can," Abbie answered, and Héctor smiled in agreement.

"Do you think it's weird that I don't really want to kiss her? All I want to do is hold her hand and be next to her. I want to do romantic things, but I don't want to do physical things."

"That's not weird at all. Plus we are literal kids— everyone else is pushing that narrative onto us. But check this out." Abbie pulled up a TED Talk on You-Tube. "Have you seen this?" She loaded the video.

"No, but I think that's one of the links Mr. Shapiro recommended I watch."

"You down to watch?" Héctor asked.

"Totally," I said.

As we watched the video together, I suddenly felt my chest tighten up. Every word that this person was saying described exactly how I had felt for as long as I could remember. The person described themselves as being non-binary. They went by they/them/their pronouns. They expressed how they didn't identify as being male or female, and how their gender journey and coming-out journey was never ending, and how gender is like a spectrum, and how it's important to honor personal experiences. They emphasized that there was no "right" time to know how you identify and that it was okay to not know. It was also okay to change your mind with how you feel you identify. They talked about how they were on the ace spectrum, which was short for *asexual*. They described some of the most common forms of attraction: mental/intellectual, romantic, and platonic, and how your attraction to people is also on a spectrum. It's not black and white. It's a rainbow.

Had I finally found my place in the world?

Words.

They began to dance inside my heart.

Words. Felt magical again.

Safe again.

Had I found my place in the world? Had I found *the words?*

Or did they find me?

Was this how relieved my mom felt when she got a diagnosis? Was this how it felt when Maya knew she was a lesbian? Or how Abbie felt when she knew she was trans? I had so many thoughts racing through my head. I was no longer feeling like I was a void. I was not an empty space.

I was everything. I had meaning. I belonged. I was non-binary and asexual.

I wanted to live my life fearlessly. I felt ready. I felt . . . all the words.

27

The next day at school I made an appointment to talk to Mr. Shapiro. I was so excited to talk to him about what I had discovered.

"I'm so happy to see you. How are you holding up? How's your mom?" Mr. Shapiro asked, leaning back in his leather chair.

"I'm great. She's doing a lot better—thanks for asking. I got to talk to her attending therapist, and she's actually coming home Monday."

"That's incredible news. How are you feeling about that?"

"I'm feeling a little bit anxious, but excited to be there for my mom, if that makes sense."

"It makes complete sense," Mr. Shapiro smiled.

"There's actually something I wanted to tell you," I said excitedly.

"Okay, I'm here. What's going on?" Mr. Shapiro said, rolling up his sleeves.

"I think I am non-binary and asexual. Yeah, that feels good to say."

"I'm so happy you have found the terminology to express your own identity. How does that make you feel?"

"Knowing how I identify? Umm . . . it feels great and scary. It feels like I'm swimming. It feels like I'm eating my favorite meal that I just learned how to cook."

"That sounds about right. Do you think knowing this will change your essay that you're working on?"

"One hundred percent," I said, pulling my hands out of my hoodie pocket.

"I'd love the opportunity to read it—with your permission, of course," Mr. Shapiro asked, fixing his bun.

"Oh, totally. I actually have to rewrite it again. But this time, I'm going to be my most authentic self. I'm not afraid anymore. I'm done hiding, and I'm going to tell my friends and my mom."

"That makes me happy. Please let me know if you need anything. I'm here to support you."

"Thanks, Mr. Shap—Mr. S. Superman."

"I could get used to that."

28

Héctor, Abbie, Jonathan, and I spent our study hall helping each other with our projects. Héctor and Jonathan were working on poetry and lyrics together. Who would have thought that Jonathan had a poet inside of him?

The days rolled by so slowly. I was busy with my friends, but was missing being with my mom. Since none of our family lived nearby, I was the one who would go in every day to feed my cats. It was a weird feeling being a house sitter at your own house.

Maya and I had started hanging out a lot more, and Héctor and Abbie would work nearly every day on new YouTube videos. Héctor was in only one episode on her channel, but he loved helping Abbie with new ideas. Abbie appointed him as the producer and even credited him at the end of each video.

When I met up with Maya the Saturday before my mom was coming home, we decided to go to the movies. The actual movies. Not a picnic at the park or picnic on my terrace. She had chosen a scary movie, but it didn't matter since we didn't really pay attention to the movie and watched each other instead.

During a make-out scene, Maya intertwined her fingers with mine and leaned in to kiss me. I immediately turned away. I didn't want that now. Or maybe ever. I wasn't sure yet. I felt like maybe I needed to know her better and form more of a bond, like they explained about people who identify as demisexual. But before I could say anything, she had stormed off. I followed her outside.

"Maya, wait," I pleaded.

"Wait? For what? For you to not be grossed out by me?" her voice shook, as tears came down from her face..

"I'm not grossed out by you," I said.

"Yeah, right," she got out.

"I'm not. I just don't want to kiss or do anything like that." I was trying to reassure her that it was me, not her.

"What does that even mean!!" she said, flailing her arms in the air. "How can you not want to kiss your own girlfriend?"

Girlfriend? Was she my girlfriend? We had never discussed labels, but I felt completely comfortable calling her my girlfriend. I just hadn't labeled it. Maybe that was the problem.

"Maya, listen to me. There's something I need to tell you. And I probably should have told you I was questioning this about myself sooner. I was afraid of what you'd think. I was afraid you might think that I didn't like you. I was afraid something like this would happen."

"What are you talking about?" Maya asked, firmly.

"Maya, I'm asexual." I continued: "I don't feel anything other than romantic attraction for you. I want you to be my girlfriend. I like you so much, so much . . ."

"That's not fair, Gabriela. You can't lead someone on and then come out as ace."

"You're right. I should have told you sooner. I mean, I guess I told you as soon as I knew? I don't know. I wasn't sure. I never meant to hurt you. I'm sorry it seemed like I was hiding it from you."

I waited for Maya to reply but she didn't. "Now what? Where does that leave us?"

"I don't know, but my Uber's going to be here in six minutes," she said, storming off and looking humiliated.

I didn't want her to know I was following her, but I watched her from the door, making sure she got into her Uber safely.

Did I just ruin everything?

Before I could even process what had happened, I realized that my mom was coming home tomorrow. I did what I always do: compartmentalize things and focus on the one thing. My mom. Besides, thinking about something I didn't have answers to got me worked up. I wanted to be happy for my mom. I wanted to be ready for her and be the person she needed.

Abbie and her dad drove me home and waited with me until my mom arrived.

My heart leaped out of my chest like a tiny little tree frog when I heard footsteps approaching the door.

Before my mom could even make it into the condo, I was hugging her.

"I missed you so much!!"

"Missed you more, butterfly." She threw her arms around me and wiped the tears from my cheeks.

"Mom . . ."

"Yes?" she said, as I clung to her arm.

"What do you love about me?"

"Hmm . . . I love your strength. And your light. And ability to never give up."

"You know what . . . I love the same thing about you."

⊙ ⊙ ⊙

"Mom . . ." I said, a few hours later, pausing an episode of *Mr. Iglesias*.

"Yes, sweetie?" She gave Cagney one last little pet, dropped him softly onto the floor, and readjusted herself.

"Do you want to die?"

"Oh gosh. No. I don't want to die. I want to live. I love living. I love seeing life through your eyes . . ."

"But . . . were you tired of living?"

"Oh, honey. It's complicated. But you deserve a response." She wrapped one arm around me. "I was very tired that day. I wanted to fall asleep. I made a choice without thinking."

"I'm asking . . . were you suicidal? And well, I don't know . . . are you feeling suicidal now?"

My mom let out a soft and quivering short sigh. "I think I have experienced suicidal ideation in the past, yes. That was not a suicide attempt." She looked deep into my eyes and wiped my tears off of my warm cheeks.

"You scared me," I said before bursting into tears again and burying my head into her arm.

"I know. I am so, so sorry."

"I mean, I'm the kid, and you're the adult. I thought I was going to lose you forever."

"I know, sweetie. I know . . ." My mom's voice cracked, and she started taking deep breaths between her sentences. "I want you to understand that I am surrounded by mental health professionals and doctors and a support group. It is not your responsibility to take care of my own mental health. You know what I mean?"

"How can I not want to take care of you?"

"You can love me. That's the care and support I need. And I will always be loving you. Okay? Deal?"

I uncurled myself and hugged my mom. "It's a deal. I've been reading more about depression in parents too. And Mr. Shapiro has been awesome. Do you think it would be okay if we checked in more on each other? Like . . . hey, how are you! Nothing too intense, just pure honesty?"

"I love that idea. So, how are you feeling, my lovely, lovely child?"

"Welll . . . ," I said, sniffling. "I am feeling happy and strong. And yep, that's it . . . for now! How are you feeling?"

"I'm feeling happier! And I want to do better at not pushing away people who care about me."

"You definitely get some bonus points for being very honest!"

"I'm trying!"

"I know . . ." I paused for a moment and let honesty take the lead and asked, "Who do you push away?"

"Hmm . . . your aunt . . . believe it or not, she's so stubborn! Ha ha! I realize it's because she loves me. And sometimes I think I push you away because I don't want you to feel this weight of responsibility. But I want to let you in and be honest with how I feel. Please trust me when I say I am going to use my professional support systems. Okay?"

"I believe ya. I'm just always gonna be loving ya!"

"And I'm always going to be loving your love and loving you."

"That's a lot of loves in one sentence, ya know?" I smiled, peering up at her.

29

It was mid-November, and the leaves were frigidly jumping off of branches. Thanksgiving was approaching, and I was thankful to be spending the holiday with my mom. I thought about what Thanksgiving looked like for other families. Did other families deal with depression too? Did other families look like ours?

Today we would start presenting our essays. Héctor had a guitar case with him, and Abbie had a huge folder with her. I had already sent my project to Mrs. Andersen. I scanned the room.

"Anyone want to volunteer to go first? If no one volunteers, we'll just go alphabetically," Mrs. Andersen tried to say threateningly.

"Me, me, me!" Abbie shouted, almost falling off her seat. It wouldn't have been her first time falling out from volunteering to go first.

"Let's see . . ." Mrs. Andersen scanned the room for more volunteers.

A few moments went by, and a hand in the back slowly shot halfway up.

"I'll do it," a familiar voice said.

I turned around and saw Jonathan's hand meekly raised.

"That's great!" Mrs. Andersen said. "Please, come up. Do you need to set up anything, first?"

"Nah, I'm good," Jonathan said, making his way up to the front of the room. "So, do we just read our thing or, like, explain?" He turned to Mrs. Andersen.

"If you want to give background info on what your project was, that could be helpful. But do whatever you feel works best for your presentation."

Jonathan cleared his throat, pulled up his pants, and started reading. The class sat frozen with silence.

Stupid
He calls you stupid
for not understanding your homework,
yells at you for not hitting a home run.
Stupid.

You fix him dinner.
He throws the dish across the table,
screams at you, and tells you it's cold,
stupid.

When he's fallen asleep
with empty beer bottles flooding the floor,
you reach down to clean up his mess.
He wakes up and hits you for being
so
stupid.
"I wasn't finished," he shouts.
"What are you, *stupid?*" he says, grabbing you
by your shirt.

Each day, you wake up and go to school.
You feel stupid.
You act stupid.
You treat people the way your dad treats you.
You wish you didn't have to be that way.

But then an unexpected friend
asks how you are.
No one asks how you are.

They pull you in for a hug
and invite you to sit with them at lunch.

You realize that you don't have to be a bully
like your dad.
Because the only thing that's stupid
is treating people how you don't want to be
treated.

The class was still frozen. Mrs. Andersen's eyes watered up, and she wiped away a tear and began to clap. Then everyone started to clap. Héctor started hooting, and Abbie got up and clapped. Soon the class was giving Jonathan a standing ovation.

Mrs. Andersen walked over to Jonathan and whispered something to him. I could only make out him saying thank you.

"Thank you, Jonathan. I can only imagine that sharing that was not easy. Thank you for trusting us enough to share. I do want to mention that *stupid* is ableist language, but for this assignment, it's important we are honest with words and conversations that impact us, and, as always, what we say here stays here. While I allowed him to continue his presentation with that word, I do want to make sure that all of us understand that we won't be using that word or any ableist language in class, okay? And, Jonathan, will you stay after class for a second so we can talk a little more about your poem? Thank you."

"We got you, Mrs. A," Héctor said.

Jonathan sat confidently in his seat and agreed with Mrs. Andersen as well. I agreed too, and soon the entire class joined in.

I turned around and gave Jonathan a smile. He smiled so wide I saw every one of his teeth.

"Anyone up to go next?" Mrs. Andersen asked.

"We'll go!" Lucy and Jessica yelled in unison.

"All right, ladies. The floor is yours," she said.

While Lucy and Jessica set up their speakers and pulled up their podcast, I leaned back in my seat, feeling suddenly petrified to share.

"You can do it," Jonathan whispered to me.

When Lucy and Jessica finished playing their podcast, everyone in class asked them a bunch of questions. Mostly, when they could be the next guest and how to start a podcast. Lucy and Jessica loved the attention and answered everyone.

I turned and saw Abbie slowly flipping through her project. She was doing a slideshow and a speech. For the first time maybe ever, though, I saw her looking sad. Abbie was always a burst of sunshine. She had taught me how to be lighter.

"What's going on, Abbie?" I asked, trying not to sound too worried.

"Nothing. I just wanted to go first to get it over with." She paused, looking away for a second. "And I guess I also wish my mom could see it. She's always gone. That's why I do the YouTube videos. I . . . sometimes it's the only way to share my life with her."

"We could record it and send it to your mom!" I said, thinking that was such a brilliant idea.

"No, I'm sick of sending her videos and pretending she was there."

A voice interrupted our conversation. "Abbie, would you like to go next?"

I felt a sadness for Abbie. I couldn't imagine what it would be like to have a mom who's only home half the year.

Abbie pushed out her chair slowly and sauntered to the front of the class. She hooked up the projector and placed each slide on. On one of her slides, a tear fell onto the projector, and she quickly wiped it off.

When she looked up, though, she saw what I was seeing too: Mrs. Andersen was talking to someone in the hall.

Then, a woman with dark eyes and black hair walked in. She was beautiful.

"Amma!" Abbie exclaimed.

"Hi, sweetie," the woman said while embracing her.

"You're here? I thought you were in Cambodia?"

The woman wiped away Abbie's tears. "I came back early—early this morning. You were my first stop back home. I know how important this project is to you."

Abbie and her mom's reunion had the class emotional. Finally, Abbie turned to the class and said, "Everyone, this is my mom. She's the one who inspires me every day. She's the real photojournalist in the family."

"That's so cool, Abs!" Héctor called, coming up and reaching out his hand to greet her mother.

"So amazing," I said, happy for her but also thinking about my mom. I wished my mom would do something like that for me.

"Hey, Abbie, what do you say you and your mom get out of here?" Mrs. Andersen winked.

"Really?" Abbie said in her animated way.

"Of course!" Mrs. Andersen smiled, motioning her head to the door. "You can present next week."

"Good because I need to make things extra perfect now that my mom is here."

As soon as Abbie and her mom left, Mrs. Andersen was asking for volunteers again. She really didn't miss a beat.

Héctor, with his guitar pick in his mouth, raised his hand.

"All right, it's all you," Mrs. Andersen announced, walking to the back of the room.

Héctor played a song on his acoustic guitar that he and Jonathan had written. Some words were in Spanish, and some were in English.

Intro
You look at me
And assume you know my whole story
Before I speak, you think I won't understand
Before I try, you think I'll fail
But you don't know me at all
Do you even care?

Look in the mirror before you look at me with your judgmental eyes
Look in the mirror before you believe any lies

Pre Chorus

Your miseducation

Is an indication

That you have no relation

To anything that doesn't concern you

It's actual

It's factual

That your mind needs to be decolonized

Realized

Conceptualized

Into something greater than yourself

Chorus

No me conocen

Pero me conozco bien

Y me gusta quien soy

Me gusta quien soy

Bridge

Stop asking where I'm really from

When you really mean

Why do I look different than you

Quit mistaking me as a thug or criminal

I'm not either

I'm not a stereotype

I'm not here for you

I'm not here for you

When he finished, everyone was clapping, and the girls were swooning over him.

Welp. It's now or never.

I raised my hand slowly, looking around to see if anyone else was too, ready to put my hand down quickly. Too late—Mrs. Andersen saw me.

"Gabriela? You ready to go?" she asked.

"Yep," I said, pulling my hands out of my hoodie pocket, scanning the class and looking for Maya.

Mrs. Andersen went to her computer and pulled up the email I had sent her; she clicked the link and put it on full screen.

Héctor hit the lights.

As a kid growing up with multiple identities, I always thought I knew who I was. I knew facts about myself and my life, but I never actually questioned how I felt about them.

It took me a while to find the language to express how I felt on the inside. I didn't have any representation to look up to. At least I didn't think I did.

This was before I met my two best friends who identified as something other than what society portrays as the norm. As I became friends with these people, I started to question my own sexual and gender identity.

All this time I thought I was being my most authentic self. I wasn't. I had been hiding. I was hiding because I honestly had no idea I could identify as something other than what I was assigned as at birth—and because I was scared.

I am a non-binary ace person. My pronouns are they/them/their, and I am proud of who I am. And from this day forward, I promise to always live as my authentic self, even if it scares me. I'm done hiding.

Héctor flipped the lights back on. My eyes were half shut, and I was afraid to see what the class was going to say.

I hear a voice say: "That's awesome, Gabriela."

Héctor turned to the class. "I'm one of the best friends by the way!" Everyone laughed.

Lucy and Jessica looked at each other, whispered something, then looked back at me.

"Would you ever want to be on our podcast?" Lucy asked.

"Yeah, we want all different types of narratives on our show," Jessica added.

"Yeah, I'd love to, but only if my two best friends can be on it too," I said, smiling at Héctor.

"For sure," they answered practically in unison.

When class was over I felt all twisted inside. I was excited to finally have been truthful to who I was, but something still didn't feel right. I realized it was because Maya hadn't been there to see it. She'd missed the last couple of classes of English. My attention to myself quickly shifted to being worried about her.

When I got home from school, I decided to text Maya and ask her to come over. My mom had been home for a few days, and things were starting to feel normal. Well, our normal.

> **ME:** hey, are you free? i want to show you something.
> **MAYA:** okay. i can come over at 7, if that's okay?
> **ME:** perfect

Before Maya came over, I finished up some pre-algebra homework and cleaned my room. It was quiet but a peaceful quiet. I could hear my mom humming and felt warmth between the walls.

"Gabriela! Maya's here!" my mom yelled from the kitchen.

"Okay, got it. Thanks!" I ran to the door, sliding in my socks. I turned before opening the door and saw my mom rinsing off some vegetables with Cagney at her feet. I'd missed this.

"Hey," I said.

"Hey," Maya replied.

"I wanted to show you something," I said, grabbing her wrist, leading her to my bedroom.

"Looks nice in here. Did you finally clean?"

"Only for you," I replied, laughing.

Maya sat at my desk chair, and I searched for my YouTube video I had shared in class that day. She looked surprised. Probably because I'd never told her I had a YouTube channel.

As the video played, Maya uncrossed her arms and loosened up. Cagney and Eliza were nuzzling her, trying to get her to snuggle. She gave in pretty easily.

The end of the video was different from what I had shown in class though.

If I could do anything differently, I would have been more honest with how I was feeling. I would have been honest with how I was questioning my own identity.

This part is going to be an apology to Maya.

Maya, I know you're watching because I just invited you over. You're probably sitting at my desk playing with your hair. Oops, now you're looking down at your nails. They look great, by the way.

Maya, I'm sorry I wasn't more upfront with you. I'm sorry I didn't tell you I was feeling confused. I'm sorry it feels like I led you on.

But the truth is—I wasn't leading you on. I truly have feelings for you.

I understand if you can't be with someone who is asexual because you're going to want something else in a relationship. That's totally understandable. But I don't want to lose you as a friend either.

Do you forgive me?

The video stopped playing, and I turned to her. "Do you forgive me, Maya? I'm truly sorry. I never meant to hurt you."

Maya looked at me, then at the ground, then back at me.

"I forgive you. I think friends are all that we can be. But I hope that next time, you'll be upfront with someone who may be interested in you. Deal?"

"Deal," I said, hugging her.

"Have you told your mom yet?" she asked.

"Um . . . yeah . . . about that."

"Well, you'll know when you're ready. But I've met your mom, and I think she'll accept you no matter what." She picked up her phone and started walking to the door.

"Wait, do you want to stay for dinner?" I wanted to have more time with her.

"Maybe another time, I'm not ready yet." There was a little distance in her voice as she put her phone in her back pocket.

"Okay, that's cool," I said, walking her to the front door.

As soon as Maya left, my mom called me to sit down and have dinner. Cagney and Eliza trailed behind me.

"So, sweetie, what's new?" my mom asked in between chews of her cranberry kale salad. "How did your presentation go, by the way?"

"It was great," I said, pushing my applesauce to the other side of the dish.

"Oh yeah! Want to elaborate?"

"Mom. I'm non-binary and asexual," I proclaimed.

My mom put down her fork. She came in closer and squeezed me.

"Oh, honey, that's wonderful. I was waiting for you to tell me on your own terms."

"What do you mean 'waiting'?" I asked.

"Well, Mr. Shapiro and I have been talking . . ."

I looked at her anxiously, wondering what she might say next.

"He didn't tell me what you were talking about, but I had asked him if he'd be comfortable sharing his own journey with you. I'd always suspected you were struggling with your own gender identity and sexuality." She continued: "And I didn't think I would be the right person to talk to. I hope that's okay." She said it with wide eyes.

"You did?" I asked, relieved and shocked.

"Of course. You're my baby. I notice everything about you. Remember when we would spend hours at the fabric store looking for suit patterns? Or when we would go to craft shows, you'd always want me to buy you bow ties."

It was funny she chose to tell me that memory.

"I love you so much, Mom," I said, wrapping my arms tighter around her. My cats wasted no time to jump in on the lovefest.

"So, are you going to show me your YouTube video?"

"Wait. What. How did you—"

"Well, I figured either you were making a video or talking to yourself!"

After I helped my mom clean up, I showed her my video. Tears filled her eyes. It really didn't take much for my mom to swell with joy.

"I'm so proud of you, baby," my mom said, wiping her eyes. Cagney licked the tears from her cheeks, and Eliza found a way to squeeze herself between us.

I couldn't wait to tell everyone at school about my mom's reaction. I felt like a weight had been lifted off of me. I was starting to feel like I belonged not only to myself but to a world that I didn't even know was there.

30

At lunch the next day I told everyone that I had come out to my mom and even showed her my YouTube video.

"That's awesome, Gabs," Héctor jumped in, cutting open an avocado.

"What's up?" Maya asked, putting her tray down.

"Gabriela came out to their mom. It went great. I can't help but feel I was part of their inspiration to do a YouTube video." Abbie nudged my elbow and smiled with excitement.

"Really?" Maya asked, smiling at me.

"Really," I said, smiling back at her.

Jonathan pulled up a seat next to me and commented on how disgusting the school lunch was, as he shoveled a chicken tender drowning in ranch into his mouth.

Abbie raised her eyebrow. "If it's so disgusting, why are you eating it?"

"I said it was disgusting; I didn't say it wasn't edible," he replied, chugging his chocolate milk.

Everyone laughed.

"Anyway," Héctor said, changing the topic, "did y'all hear about the dance? What are we thinking?"

"Pass." Abbie shrugged.

"I don't know, I think it would be fun," Maya said with a smile.

Jonathan was too engrossed in his lunch to reply.

"Yeah," I agreed. "It could be fun."

"We should all go. Like as a group," Abbie declared, looking at Jonathan.

"I thought you just said 'pass,'" I said.

"I did. True. Great listening. But I can change my mind, can't I?" Abbie replied, pushing her crumbs to the floor.

"Okay, so then it's decided. We're going to the dance together!" Héctor called as he burped.

Everyone cracked up. Burping would never stop being gross and funny. I guess we were going to the dance. I had never been to a dance. I had never been to a dance with an ex-girlfriend . . . former crush . . . er, words are hard. But I was excited to be going with a bunch of friends.

This would either be awesome or awkward. Maybe a little bit of both.

31

As I sat in Spanish class, I gazed out of the window. I watched two birds fighting for a piece of bread. The wind was blowing hard, and the garden we'd planted last year in Earth Science was covered in brown leaves. I wondered if nature ever got sad or exhausted. Each year flowers would bloom, but did they know their fate? That by the time winter came, they'd be buried under leaves? Did they know that they'd pop back up in the spring?

Mrs. Dickens interrupted my thoughts and slid a test onto my desk. I had totally forgotten we had a test.

I turned through the test papers. The first part was fill-in-the-blank, the second part was matching, and then there was a section of questions. The last portion of the test was an essay. I started with the essay portion first.

When we finished the test, Maya scooted her desk closer to mine.

"How do you think you did?" she asked.

"I didn't even study. I totally forgot we had a test today." I was disappointed in myself.

"I'm sure you'll be fine. You're practically better at Spanish than Mrs. Dickens."

"I guess . . ." My voice trailed off.

"Hey, I'm excited for the dance Saturday. I kind of think it's super corny, but it could be fun. Life's too short not to have fun."

"Yeah." She was right. Life was too short, and I was still sitting around moping and feeling sorry for myself. I spent too much time thinking about things I couldn't change. I couldn't change that my mom had depression, and I didn't think I could change that I didn't feel quite right in my body. But the thing that I *could* change was my ability to put into words how I felt. And now I had a group of friends—and even my mom and Mr. Shapiro—to talk to. But I think all that sounded a lot simpler than it was.

When I got home from school, my mom was on the terrace watering the plants. Good thing she didn't have a regular job, or we'd be in trouble.

"Hey, sweetie, you hungry for a snack? I got some warm pita bread and some freshly-picked veggies."

"Sure," I said. Cagney trailed behind me, hoping I'd drop a crumb.

"What's wrong, butterfly?"

I should have realized that one-word answers would send an alert to my mom's brain.

"Nothing. I just feel weird."

"Weird how?"

"Well, there's a school dance that I'm going to go to with everyone, and Maya's coming too." At that moment, I realized that my mom didn't even know that I had been sort of dating Maya. She had been away in rehab.

"So, what's wrong with Maya coming?" my mom asked, spooning a glob of hummus onto the plate.

"I kind of was dating her," I said quietly.

"Oh, honey!" She hugged me with her spoon full of hummus in her hand.

"Watch the hummus," I said, smiling up at her.

"Are you still friends?" Now she was licking off the rest of it from the spoon.

"Yeah."

"That's great," my mom said, looking into the distance. "I don't think I could even remember my middle school boyfriend's name if you paid me."

But the thing was, I wasn't really worried about going with Maya. She and I were friends, and I was actually feeling fine about that.

I was worried, I realized, about what I was going to wear. I wasn't really sure what my gender expression was yet. I still didn't know how I wanted to appear on the outside.

I was still worrying about what other people would think of me.

32

At lunch the next day, they were serving tater tots. Héctor piled a massive stack onto his plate and poured cheese, jalapeño peppers, and diced tomatoes onto it.

"Hold up." He ran over to the lunch lady. "Everyone close your eyes," he said as he returned and placed the plate back onto the table. "Okay, now open! I present to you . . . totchos!"

"Totchos?" Jonathan asked.

"Tater tots and nachos equals totchos," Héctor said, impressed with himself.

I was low-key impressed too and dug in.

"So, what's the review?" Héctor asked as he pulled a tot from the pile, attached to about a mile of cheese. "Five stars?"

"Eleven out of ten," Abbie said, stuffing her face.

"Yeah, it's amazing, Héctor," I agreed.

"So, enough about me," Héctor went on. "Are ya'll hype for the dance?"

"I guess?" I replied.

"Well, I have something that may make you more hype," Héctor said, squirting some hot sauce onto his plate. "My brother is going to be DJ'ing."

"I had no idea your brother was a DJ. That's pretty cool!" Abbie said. "And you know me, it takes a lot for me to be impressed. I'm like Shania Twain but not. I'll still have to sign off on the track list to be completely impressed." She chuckled at her own wit.

"Yeah, he's actually been DJ'ing for a while now. The night that he was jumped . . ." Héctor paused. "It was his first gig here in Brooklyn." Héctor let out a big sigh and continued. "But you know, Arturo, he never quits, no matter what."

Before anyone could reply, Héctor got up from his seat and quickly left.

"That's rough," Jonathan said.

"Yeah . . . his brother has been through a lot," I said.

"He's brave to keep DJ'ing," Jonathan added.

"To be fair, Jonathan, what do you know about brave?" Abbie interrupted. "You've just recently decided you're a good person. And I let it slide because I felt bad for you. What were you doing before you even met us? You don't have the right to call us brave. We don't want to be called BRAVE! We just want to live!" She bit her thumb nail so hard the polish chipped off, and grabbed her bag.

"I didn't mean to upset anyone. I won't say something like that again," Jonathan said, bowing his head down.

"Jonathan, just say sorry and then show us you're sorry by your actions. It's simple," Abbie said sternly.

"I did."

"No, you did not. You didn't say those words."

"What's the difference? You know my intention and that I didn't mean it that way or to be rude. I am sorry. I really am."

"It's about the impact of the words. Your intention is whatever. Anyway, thanks for finally saying sorry. Have those be the first two words next time. Can you see why that may not be the best thing to say?" Abbie asked, as she started to briskly walk away.

"For sure. No one wants to be called brave for existing," Jonathan replied.

"Exactly. We just want to live. Be respected. Our existence shouldn't be seen as something so brave or radical automatically. Like, yeah, we are awesome though," I said, before running after Abbie.

33

The next morning, I woke up with the sun playfully bouncing off of my hair. When I spent a lot of time in the sun, my hair would show speckles of blond and red.

As I opened my eyes, I heard the sounds of Shakira trickling through the apartment. My mom knew how much I loved her. When I first learned about Shakira, I begged my mom to dye my hair red like hers. She seemed more excited than I was. When I got to school the next day with my new red hair, not everyone was as excited about it as my mom and I. Some people even made fun of it. But the next day, the girl who had been picking on my hair came into school with her hair fire-engine red. Everyone kept complimenting her. That day after school I told my mom I wanted to change it back. My mom didn't ask any questions and made a hair appointment for me.

Old-school Shakira was my favorite. I mean, I could appreciate Shakira's crossover to American pop music, but I still had a special love for red-haired rock star Shakira—jet-black hair, *Pies Descalzos* Shakira.

"I don't know the words, so you'll have to help me sing," my mom said, popping her head into my room.

I picked up my brush and used it as a microphone and started belting Shakira's hit song, "Estoy Aqui."

"There it is!" my mom yelled, dancing.

I jumped off my bed and pushed my hair out of my face.

"So, what do you have planned for today?" my mom asked when the song died down, cradling Eliza like a baby. Eliza gave her a death stare and then her aloof stare and then finally her body gave in, a body movement only people with cats can read. It read: I've given up, and this isn't so bad. Hold me, human; love me, human.

"I was thinking of visiting Héctor at work. The school dance is tonight, and I still haven't decided what to wear. Grr. Clothes are frustrating."

"I see no lie there. I hear you, butterfly. Remember that clothes are fabric, and I'm a seamstress! That all sounds good, butterfly . . ." my mom trailed off as she danced her way out of my room.

When I got to Jupiter, Héctor was re-stocking CDs and glancing down, trying to hide that he was on his phone.

"Hey!" I said, hoping he wasn't upset from yesterday at lunch.

"Hey, Gabs," he said without stopping his work.

"Excited for the dance?" I asked.

"Yeah, for sure. I was just texting Arturo some tracks I want him to play." Héctor finished putting away the last CD from his crate and turned to me. He continued: "I told him he had to open with 'Techno Cumbia' by Selena. Anything for Selenas, chu kno?"

"Claro . . . so, um . . . ," I began, looking down and biting my nails.

"What's up?" he said.

"Do you think you could help me pick out an outfit?" I finally asked.

"DUUUUUDE!!! Wait, are you chill with 'dude'?"

"Yeah, it doesn't bother me."

"Cool, cool, cool. Just tell me when it does, and you'll never hear me say it again. Oh, Gabs. Have I told you how lucky you are to have me? I'm almost done here. Meet me back here in thirty minutes?"

"Awesome, okay!" I said, gushing with excitement.

For the next thirty minutes, I wandered around outside, window shopping. I had never really noticed clothing store display windows until today. I guess shops around here knew that schools were busy having awkward middle school dances and took the opportunity to advertise as much as possible.

The mannequins in each shop were so heteronormative. I felt proud knowing more language from a community I was learning to be a part of. Everywhere I looked I saw a male-presenting mannequin in a suit and a female-presenting mannequin in a sparkly pink dress.

Until finally, I walked past a shop called One Size Doesn't Fit All. Points for the creative name. I walked in and immediately saw Pride Flags and LGBTQIA+ books. Before I could make out any of the titles, I heard a familiar voice call my name.

"Gabriela?"

I turned around to see David smiling at me. "How are you? I haven't seen you since, well, you know . . ." His voice trailed off.

"Yeah," I said. "I'm fine. I'm actually just waiting for Héctor. We have a school dance tonight, and he's gonna help me pick out an outfit."

"Oh yeah, I know. Arturo is DJ'ing. Unfortunately, I have to work, but I'd totally crash it if I could. Are school dances still as awkward as they were back in my day? Remember, I'm old."

I wouldn't know; I've never gone to any, I thought.

"You're not old. You're, like, twenty-something. If anything . . . wise? And yep," I said, wishing I actually knew the answer. No one had ever invited me to a dance, and I'd never really had a group of friends to go with.

As we were talking, my eyes focused on some long undershirts hanging from a rack.

"What are those?" I asked David.

"Oh, those are binders. A lot of our queer costumers buy them."

I remembered Mr. Shapiro telling me that he used to wear a binder. I hadn't really thought about my chest. Whenever I did, I quickly pushed the thought out of my head and found comfort in my daydream. *Chest-less daydreams, in the tune of "Care-less Whisper," but also not because ew, but l o l *

"I see . . ."

"Yeah, sometimes people experience gender dys-phoria, and our binders make them feel more comfortable."

"What's dysphoria?" I asked. Mr. Shapiro had never used that word before.

"There's no one way to describe what gender dysphoria is, since everyone experiences it differ-ently and it's a spectrum," David explained. "If I had gender dysphoria, I may even find getting dressed stressful because the clothes I want to wear don't complement my body shape and how I feel when I look at myself. But I identify as a cis male and I was assigned male at birth, so I while I listen and sup-port my friends and consumers, I don't experience that."

"Okay," I said, overwhelmed. I looked down and scanned my outfit. I was wearing my infamous over-sized hoodie and sweatpants. Kind of my uniform. Or cage.

"Do you think I could try on a binder?" I asked, biting my lower lip.

"Of course. Do you mind what color? Half binder, or tank binder?" David asked, picking out a few.

"I'll try on whatever." I looked around to see if anyone was watching.

"Awesome, why don't you try these on for starters?" he said, handing me a few binders. "I'll be right here if you need anything." He smiled warmly.

When I got into the dressing room there was a full-length mirror at the back of the door. I had never really looked at myself in a full-length mirror before. I always avoided them because the person I saw staring back at me wasn't me.

I quickly took off my sweatshirt, my undershirt, and sports bra and squeezed into the first binder he'd given me. Was this what a caterpillar felt like when they were trotting around on Earth before becoming a butterfly? Inch by inch, I rolled down the binder.

"It's going to feel tight but not so tight that you can't breathe," I heard David say from the other side of the door.

I slowly pulled down the binder and adjusted it so it felt more comfortable, while still avoiding eye contact with the mirror. I reached for my shirt I'd thrown in the corner and put it on over my head. I waited a minute, then opened one eye.

Then my other eye, then I closed my other eye. I took a deep breath. Slicked my hair back with my eyes closed and scrunched up my nose. *You can do this, you can do this*, I pumped myself up.

I opened my eyes and stared directly at the mirror.

It was me.

I finally saw myself again.

I hadn't seen myself since before the *P* word. Puberty.

Tears immediately filled my eyes. I guess I'm a crier like my mom too. "How's it going in there?" David asked. I opened the door to show him. "It looks great. How do you feel?" David said, grinning at me.

"I feel like me." I smiled so big, I felt the corners of my mouth open like a butterfly.

"Perfection," David replied, smiling and walking back to the front.

When I went up to the counter to pay, I asked David if it was okay that I wore it out, and he was cool with it. As I searched for some cash, I noticed a bunch of pronoun pins next to the register.

"Can I add this too?" I asked.

"It's on the house. First binders always come with a free pin." I knew that couldn't be true, but I thanked him anyway.

Walking out of the store, I felt closer to myself than I had ever felt in my life. I couldn't wait to show Héctor.

"Hey, dude, perfect timing. Where'd ya end up going?" Héctor asked as he waved bye to his dad.

"I was over at One Size Doesn't Fit All."

"Oh, nice. David works over there. Did you get anything?" We started walking to his house.

"Look again," I said as I stopped walking.

"Sweet, is that a new pin? I have a few too. It looks great."

"Notice anything else?"

"Hmm . . . no?"

"I'm wearing a binder!" I exclaimed.

"I kind of figured, but I didn't want to assume. Plus, I wanted you to say it," he said, grinning.

"Dude!" I yelled, punching his arm softly.

"So? How's it feel?"

"It feels like me."

"That's what's up!" Héctor said, giving me a side hug.

When we got to Héctor's house, no one was at home. His mom was a nurse and worked odd hours, his dad was closing up Jupiter tonight, and his brother was teaching some kids downtown how to DJ and would be meeting us all at the dance.

"So, I was thinking about what you could wear tonight. Wow, I feel like Tan from *Queer Eye* right now. But like me, obvi."

"Okay, what is it?" I asked curiously.

"Sooo . . . ," Héctor said, pushing through clothes in his closet, "I was thinking you could wear this."

I looked up to find him holding a purple three-piece suit. My eyes glistened, but I didn't say anything. I didn't have to.

"My brother wore this to my cousin's baby shower a few years ago, and it doesn't fit him anymore. I tried it, and I gotta be honest, I can't really rock it. But I know you could. Wanna try it on?" he suggested enthusiastically.

"A purple suit?" I said.

"Actually, it's periwinkle. Come on, try it on." He was beaming at me.

"All right, all right. Give me a sec."

Héctor left the room, and I put on the pieces of the suit one by one. He was right. I did rock it.

I opened the door, and Héctor literally squealed.

"Dude. This is a look! Hold up, let me fix one thing." Héctor bent down and folded each pant leg a few times.

"There we go. Now, that's THE look." He stepped back, proud of himself. "So, what do you think?"

"Wow . . . I . . . I love it." I was smiling uncontrollably.

"You're welcome," he said happily.

"Gracias!" I hugged him.

"De nada!" he said, returning the hug.

"Okay, I'm gonna run home and take a quick shower. I also want to show my mom. Meet you at Abbie's, okay?" I said to Héctor. He didn't respond; he was still gazing at the suit. "Héctor!" I said, nudging him.

"Of course. I'll see you there," he replied, clearly still impressed with his styling advice.

34

When I got back home, my mom was finishing up her quilt for my cousin's baby. It was beautiful.

"That looks gorgeous, Mom," I told her, sitting on the arm of the sofa.

"Thank you, sweetheart," she said, transfixed on her project.

I got up from the sofa. "I want to show you something."

"What is it?" she replied, her eyes still fixated on the quilt.

"Look," I said, standing in front of her in my periwinkle three-piece suit.

"My butterfly. It's fabulous!" She stood, examining the suit like the seamstress she is. "Where did you get a suit like this? You know I could whip one up for you."

I hadn't asked my mom to sew something for me in a long time. I hadn't wanted to cause any unneeded stress, but now somehow, it felt like my not asking had disappointed her. It was hard to know what the right thing to do was a lot of the time.

"I know, and I would have loved that, honestly. It was totally random. Héctor just had it lying around. I wasn't even sure I wanted to go to the dance."

"Oh, I understand. It's quite dapper."

"Thank you, thank you very much," I said, fixing my collar and bowing.

"Seriously, it's perfect. It's so you!" My mom kissed me on the forehead.

"Thanks, Mom."

"Will you let me take a selfie of you?"

It's just a picture, not a selfie, I said to myself, wanting to correct her. "Of course!"

My mom jumped into the picture with me, smiling. It was probably the happiest I had seen her in a while.

"Now, shouldn't you be getting ready?" She smirked at me.

"Yes!" I said, making my way to the bathroom. Before I closed the door, I called, "Hey, Mom, can you do one long braid down my back like you used to?"

"Of course, sweetie, whatever you want," she answered, holding her hand to her heart.

"Oh and, Mom," I said, poking my head through the door. "I love you. Thanks for accepting me."

"I've always accepted you, my butterfly, and I always will."

After I got out of the shower and my mom braided my hair and told me how long it was getting, she drove me to Abbie's house.

When I walked in, everyone was in the living room drinking lemonade. Abbie's mom offered me a glass, before I even had a chance to sit down.

"Gabriela! SLAY! You LOOK amazing!!" Abbie screamed. She screamed so loud and high pitched even the lemonade had a reaction.

"Yeah, totally, you look awesome," Jonathan agreed in an indoor voice.

"You look great," Maya said, motioning me to sit next to her. "You look comfortable."

"I feel comfortable," I said, smiling.

"But, Gabs," Héctor went on, "we gotta find more outfits for you! You can't wear suits and sweats all year round. Deal?" He grinned.

"Deal." I beamed back.

After we all finished getting ready, Mrs. Mehta said we should get going. We piled into her car and headed to the dance.

35

When we got to the dance, Arturo was already in the DJ booth playing and there were only three people dancing on the dance floor. Héctor ran up to the booth to probably inspect his brother's track list and strongly suggest some tunes.

Mrs. Andersen was ushering people in, and Mr. Shapiro was on snack bar duty. I felt so confident in my suit that I walked up to Mr. Shapiro to show off my new threads. He fist-bumped me and smiled as I turned around to join my friends.

As I walked back, a few people snickered at me.

"Nice suit. Where's the funeral?" one person said.

"You look like a huge lesbo," another person muttered.

When I got back to my group, I blurted out to everyone what people were saying about me. "Maybe this wasn't a good idea," I said, holding back tears. "I should just go home,"

"What? No way!" Héctor insisted. "Don't let anyone tell you that you don't belong. You love your outfit, and you're here with your friends. Please stay."

Abbie swallowed the ice she was chewing and added, "Who's saying it? They literally said *lesbo*? *At least* be original, people! Where are they? I just wanna talk." She crunched the plastic cup in her hand.

I laughed. I didn't think Abbie realized it, but she could be pretty meme-y. Or maybe she did, and the joke was on us the entire time. I wouldn't put it past her.

"Listen, don't let anyone make you feel inferior without your consent."

"Eleanor Roosevelt?" I said, raising my eyebrow.

"No. Abbie Roosevelt," she joked, then continued: "Don't let a bunch of people you don't even know affect you. It's not worth your time. Trust me. Focus on the being here with us. Not to mention, your identity is none of their business."

"Yeah, Gabs, remember how excited you were when you first put on the suit? You're not their problem. They are their own problem. Don't sweat them. Plus, I already nominated you for Best Dressed, so you can't leave."

"There's a Best Dressed competition?" I asked suspiciously.

"No, but if there was one, you'd win it. Now come on, stay," Héctor persisted.

"All right, all right, I'll stay!" I said, shaking off any negative feelings.

"I'm glad you're staying," Maya said softly.

"Anyone want some punch?" Héctor asked.

"Or to get punched?" Abbie said, still giving the two people a death stare.

"Abs . . . ," Héctor said, giving her arm a little squeeze.

"I'm just saying. I'm watching. I'm ready."

"I'll take some," I said.

"Me too," Jonathan replied.

"Me three," Abbie echoed.

"I don't think I have enough hands for that. Wanna help me?"

Abbie, Jonathan, and Héctor disappeared into the crowd, leaving me and Maya alone. We hadn't been alone together since I'd showed her my video.

"I'm really happy you're embracing who you are, Gabriela," Maya said gently, pushing her braids to the side.

"Me too," I murmured, looking down at my Docs.

"You wanna dance?" She asked me in such an effortlessly cool way.

"Are you sure?"

"If I wasn't sure, I wouldn't ask. Now, let's dance." She pulled me in closer. We held onto each other and slowly danced to "Don't Let Me Down," by Solange. I looked over at Arturo, giving him an *I saw that, and I approve* nod.

Maya rested her head on my shoulder and whispered: "I'm glad we can still be friends."

"Me too."

Before the song ended the two people who had made the comments earlier came back to taunt me some more.

"Oh my god, so you actually are a lesbo," one of them said. "Gross."

"Two little lezzies sitting in a tree," the other one sang, thinking they were clever.

I let go of Maya and turned to them. But before I could speak, Abbie and Jonathan had swooped in.

"Are you for real? You're going to harass someone for dancing? Do you know how homophobic you sound right now?"

Before Abbie finished, there was a crowd of kids surrounding us. The music stopped, and teachers were making their way through the crowd.

"You know, being a bully is one thing, but being a homophobic turd is another. Why don't you get out of here and leave all of us alone!" Jonathan yelled.

The two kids pushed their way through the crowd, searching for the exit as Mr. Shapiro quickly followed them.

"Thanks for sticking up for us," I said, feeling protected by friends but still super creeped out by what I'd experienced.

"Don't worry about it. Are you okay?" Jonathan asked with genuine concern.

"Meh. It was super gross."

"I'm so sorry, Gabriela."

"Thanks."

"And what they were saying wasn't right," Jonathan declared, puffing out his chest.

"I appreciate that, and thanks for asking me if I was okay," I said, giving him a hug. He hugged me as if no one had ever hugged him before. *Literally.*

"But let's be honest," Abbie pronounced, brushing off her shoulders. "We all know it was me that scared them faster than seeing a FaceApp After photo."

"For sure, Abs. You're bossy and flossy," Héctor said, then he pointed at his brother.

"TKN" by ROSALÍA and Travis Scott started playing and we all danced, remembering the choreography.

Even the teachers joined in. The energy was magical.

I didn't want the night to end.

36

The following Monday after the dance, Mrs. Andersen and Mr. Shapiro pulled us all aside and told us that they had suspended the two kids who'd been harassing Maya and me. Mr. Shapiro even invited our parents to come talk to him the next day.

"First and foremost, I want to offer my sincere apologies for this situation ever happening. Our school's zero-tolerance policy is flawed. I'll be the first to admit that. I want to work with you to try to come up with more strategies to prevent this from happening again."

Even though it seemed like Mr. Shapiro had a speech prepared, Abbie took the opportunity to jump in between one of his deep sighs. "Listen, Mr. Shapiro, I think it's awesome that you're saying all of this. And you're right, the zero-tolerance-for-bullying policy doesn't actually work."

"Abbie . . ." Her mom leaned in with a stern look on her face.

She continued: "I mean honestly, research supports what I just said. The fact of the matter is telling someone to stop being a bully isn't going to stop them. Look at Jonathan, for instance—no offense, Jonathan. Bullying isn't an individual problem, it's a family problem, a community problem. You put it all on us, the kids, when really it's important that students AND parents are involved."

Abbie finished, letting out a deep breath. She bit her lower lip nervously. I'd never seen her visibly nervous before.

"You're right," Mr. Shapiro said. "Everything you said was spot on. So, where do we go from here?"

"Well, Mike—can I call you Mike?" Abbie said, testing her limits.

"Unfortunately, I'm still Mr. Shapiro to you," he replied, trying not to crack a smile.

"Well, Mr. Shapiro, it's so funny you should ask. My friends and I have decided that we want to create a series of vlogs that will help bring about awareness to LGBTQIA+ issues and to help stop bullying."

We all shot her a look, since this was the first time any of us had heard of this plan.

Abbie continued: "At my old school I worked with the school principal and recorded content for our school, so they could learn about me and my own experiences. Each video contained a lot of information that helped kids understand who I was rather than judge who I was."

"I was hesitant at first," Mrs. Mehta interjected, as she could see Mr. Shapiro feeling unsure about Abbie's suggestion. "But her videos truly created not only a safe space for Abbie and those who identified as trans or even gender nonconforming or nonbinary, but they opened up a dialogue for kids and promoted a strong sense of empathy among her peers. Their parents too. Her videos were also used to help her teachers and faculty become more informed."

"Well," Mr. Shapiro said, leaning forward out of his chair, "I think we have a lot to discuss. Let's plan to meet after Thanksgiving," he promised, holding out his hand to shake our parents' hands. He reached out to give us all a handshake, but we elbow-bumped him instead.

37

The next couple of days were half days, and teachers didn't really plan much for us to do. The day of Thanksgiving, my mom picked me up early and we rocked out to music until we got to my aunt's house on Long Island.

I had been thinking of the thousands of ways I could come out to my family since the moment I'd come out to my mom. Coming out to my mom had taken a lot of courage, but coming out to my family was another story. We only saw them a few times a year, and let's just say, I was probably the weird cousin everyone says they have.

As I sketched trees and scenery we drove by, my phone vibrated. I had texted everyone earlier, telling them I planned to come out but wasn't sure how to.

ABBIE: I say go for it. Whenever. create your time!

JONATHAN: wait for a moment when they're, like, talking about politics or trans issues.

HÉCTOR: well you know, I don't really like to talk about politics in group chats . . . jk, but yeah, Jonathan has a point. families will always talk politics. totally unavoidable.

MAYA: wait for another family member to come out or be questioned why they don't have a significant other yet. haha, that's what happened last year when my cousin, jackson, came out.

When we got to my Aunt Susie's house, she was knee deep in cooking as my Uncle George was plopped in front of the TV, watching sports and listening to Kacey Musgraves.

"If I had a free hand, I'd give you a huge hug," my aunt said, giving me an air kiss.

"Need a hand, sis?" my mom called from down the stairs as she dropped our suitcases into the guest room.

"No, no. I'm fine! I just have a husband who is more connected to sports than the profound spirit of togetherness and FAMILY," she called back, directing her voice at Uncle George. He didn't even flinch.

"How 'bout you help set the table," she said, motioning me to start collecting dishes.

As we set the table, my aunt asked how I was doing in school. We chitchatted for a few minutes until the door rang. I couldn't say I was upset that the spotlight was off me.

The door flung open, and my cousins Sofia and Kelly burst in. They sure knew how to make an entrance. I moved to the back of the room as they made their rounds to greet everyone.

As everyone gathered around the TV, I sat at the table, eyeing the antipasto. My Aunt Susie called out, saying the food was ready. I was ready too. Finally, everyone made it to their seats and started digging in.

"So, Sofia, any handsome men in your life?" Aunt Susie gushed.

"Susie, if she wanted to bring up her romantic life, she would have," Uncle George said, glaring at my aunt.

"I'm actually seeing someone. I've actually been seeing them for the last year," Sofia replied in between bites.

"Who is he?!" Aunt Susie cried, inching her way to the edge of her seat.

"She," Sofia corrected Aunt Susie.

This was it. We had officially entered the queer zone. I could totally go into telling everyone I was non-binary and ace.

"Oh, well, that's sweet, honey," Aunt Susie continued as she guzzled her drink down. "When are we going to meet *her*?"

"I'm not sure yet. She's not out, and I wouldn't want to scare her away inviting her to meet my dysfunctional family," Sofia said jokingly.

Before my family bounced to the next topic, I cleared my throat, cracked my neck, and said: "I have something I also want to share too. I'm non-binary. My pronouns are they/them/their. I'm also asexual." I felt the blood go to my head and my shoulders get tense.

My mom grabbed my hand and smiled. While the rest of the table went radio silent, all you could hear was Molly the dog scrambling from under the table to pick up any fallen food.

"So, you're gay," my uncle said, chewing a roll and reaching for another one.

"No. I'm ace. My gender identity has nothing to do with my sexual orientation," I said, raising my voice.

"City girl, listen to you and all these new-age terms. I mean, sure, gay, we get. But this? That just isn't a thing." Aunt Susie's eyes widened as she took another serving of salad and turned to my mom. "Is this what they're teaching in school these days?"

"Gabriela does not identify as being female or male. Their pronouns are they/them/their, so calling Gabriela a girl is devaluing what they just said." My mom slammed her glass down on the table. I'd never seen her this upset before.

"Isn't this a little much for a dinner conversation?" my cousin Kelly said, looking up from her phone. "Besides, how do you know that? You're, like, ten."

"I'm almost thirteen," I said under my breath.

"I think we're done here," my mom said, throwing her napkin onto the table and grabbing my hand, leading me downstairs to our guest room.

"Come on, kiddo, pack your things. We're going home."

"But, Mom. I'm fine. I guess." I wasn't fine. I was humiliated. How could my family, the one I'd known my whole life, act like what I said didn't matter, that who I was didn't matter? But even still, I wanted to stay. I deserved to stay.

My mom kneeled in front of me and pushed my hair out of my face. "Listen, my butterfly, I will not subject you to anyone who doesn't accept you and see what I see in you." She was holding back tears. As she continued to pack, she said, fuming, "I mean, they can understand Sofia having a girlfriend, but when it comes to you, they act like what you're saying is gibberish?"

Before I could stop myself, I was speaking. "Mom, I don't want to leave." I said it as my mom was still muttering under her breath. "Mom! This isn't your decision to make. I don't want to leave." I let it out without fumbling over any word. I knew exactly what I needed to say and I said it.

"Sweetheart—"

"Ever since I can remember, we've always been finding reasons to leave. I don't want to leave this time." My mom had a history of running away from anything that didn't fit into what she had planned. And when I came into the picture, I had to run away with her too. As my mom continued to fold her clothes, we heard a knock at the door.

"Can I speak to Gabriela alone?" It was my Aunt Susie.

My mom glanced at me, asking me with her eyes if it was okay. I nodded, and she went back upstairs. I sat in the computer chair as my aunt came in and waited for her to say the first words.

"It wasn't right of us not to listen to you and to dismiss what you were saying. We want to understand. It's just hard for us," Aunt Susie said, cleaning her glasses on her shirt. "It's true, I've never heard these terms before. But I looked them up, and I'll do my best to understand and listen to you—and, of course, respect you."

Sofia bounced down the stairs with phone in hand, "Yeah, goober, we got your back."

I didn't reply. I was waiting for an apology. I wanted to hear the words *I am sorry*. I was waiting for real acceptance—maybe not a parade, but acceptance. But I knew I probably wouldn't get either of these things.

Still, this was more than I had imagined she would do, and I accepted it for what it was. Even though I knew I deserved more.

When we got back to the table, tea was being served and boxes of once-overflowing pastries had been opened and half consumed.

My uncle cut a cannoli and offered me the bigger piece.

This was *his* peace offering. I took it.

I wasn't expecting everyone to understand right away. I mean, it took me a while to understand, and it was happening to me. I guess I just wished they were more open to talking about it with me.

38

The next morning, we got up before the sun could greet us hello and drove back home. As we turned off our exit, my mom's phone rang.

"Would you see who it is, butterfly?"

I fumbled for her phone in her purse—it read SISTER CELL.

"It might be important; can you put it on speaker and hold it up?" My mom tucked her hair behind her ear. She was a very cautious driver; she'd never even gotten a parking ticket, as she loved to remind me whenever I suggested she slow down or warned her about being too close to the car in front of us.

"Hey, sis, is Gabriela there?" my aunt's voice sounded.

"I hope so. Or that would mean my mom left me in Long Island," I replied jokingly into the phone.

"Thanks for telling me I was on speaker phone, Ange."

"You know me!"

"I do. That's the problem."

"Funny!"

"All right. We get it. You're sisters and you love to banter!" I laughed.

"I was actually calling to talk to you, Gabriela . . ."

I quickly took the phone and put it off speaker.

"Listen, Gabriela, I wanted to apologize for the way we—err, I acted the other day. I guess you kind of caught me off guard. But that's not your problem. It's my problem. I want to be better. I am sorry."

"I forgive you, Aunt Susie. Thanks for calling." My heart swelled with happiness. It wasn't perfect, but it was progress.

As soon as I hung up the phone, my mom gave my hand a squeeze.

"Your aunt loves you, sweetie." My mom cradled my face with one hand, still looking at the road. "I love you."

"Love you too, Momma mia."

Later in the day, Maya called me and told me to look outside. Who calls people anymore? I guess she was sort of forced to since I wasn't answering any of her texts.

I sauntered over to the window and looked outside. Héctor, Abbie, Jonathan, and Maya were sitting in Héctor's brother's car, but David was in the driver's seat.

"Come on, David's gonna drive us!" Maya shouted up at me.

"Where are we going?" I called.

"You never really were good at the meaning of surprises. Just get in." She smiled, beckoning me to join them. Héctor squeezed in next to Abbie, and Maya and Jonathan were in the front with David.

"Anyone feeling like REZZ?" David asked when I got in, pleased with himself by knowing who REZZ, Alison Wonderland, and even SOPHIE was. I guess knowing musical artists came with the territory of dating a DJ, but I already knew them too. So maybe you didn't have to date someone to learn something.

As David and Jonathan jammed out to Arturo's mix, Maya, Héctor, and Abbie were babbling about the latest feud between YouTube creators.

Before pulling up to get Uncle Louie G's Italian ices, Abbie asked how seeing my family was.

"It was weird, but I think it can only get better from here."

"Definitely," Abbie said, racing to the counter.

It was in that moment I realized no matter what happened in my life, I really would have friends who would support me and be there for me. Friends I could be goofy with, friends who saw me for who I was, and loved me no matter what. If that wasn't belonging, I didn't know what was.

39

The next day after school, Mr. Shapiro called us all back in as he'd promised before Thanksgiving break.

"I've given your proposal a lot of thought, and I'd like to give it the green light."

"YESS!!" we all basically said in unison.

"But before you begin, I'd like you to write out each episode and work with Mrs. Andersen and myself so we can try to incorporate it into the curriculum. How does that sound?"

"When can we start?" Héctor asked.

"I'd like to start it next fall. I want to make sure that we are all on the same page and will create something that will be long lasting and not rushed."

"I guess you're right," Abbie moaned with disappointment.

"Sometimes," Mr. Shapiro said with a grin. "And, before you go. I wanted to suggest that we use the vlogs as a tool during monthly workshops."

"What?" we all said, confused.

"What I mean is Mrs. Andersen and I talked, and we want to roll out a new initiative. The vlogs are only part of it. We've put out some feelers, and other schools and organizations are interested in helping us create a series of workshops. Counselors and other school administrators will help lead discussions with students AND PARENTS. We'll collaborate and use your tools to lead the workshops. Your input is what will make this successful. How's that sound?"

"So let me get this gay . . . you're saying that our faces will be used all over the city?" Abbie squealed. "Why Mr. Shapiro, I thought you'd never ask. I've been waiting for my close-up."

"But first, I need everyone to sign off on this. Here are some papers for you and your parental units or caregivers," Mr. Shapiro said.

We all looked at one another and grabbed the papers.

"Of course!" we practically all said in unison.

We walked out of his office feeling really excited to start planning. When I told my mom the good news, she said she was going to send a mass email with our first video to our whole family. She even mentioned making custom outfits for us. I loved it.

40

The next couple of months felt like a dream. I would go over to Abbie's with everyone to help plan our vlogs almost every day.

As spring gracefully bloomed into summer, we all gushed over our plans. Abbie was going to a four-week photography camp in California. Héctor was going to guitar camp, and Maya was going to theatre camp downtown. As for Jonathan, he was moving with his mom to his grandparents'. I would be spending half of the summer volunteering at the animal shelter and the other half of the summer with family in Long Island.

The first day of summer greeted me like an old friend. Homemade blueberry pancakes took over my senses, the dancing sun fluttered into my room, and Eliza was flicking her tail in my face. Who needed an alarm when you have a cat's tail?

As I slid out of bed, the folky sounds of Brett Dennen greeted me at my door. My mom and I were starting to show real signs of being Brett Dennen's number one fans, but don't tell Stevie Nicks that.

I put on the clothes that I had hung up over my door the night before, put my pin onto my shirt, straightened my back, and looked into my full-length mirror. My mouth bloomed into a smile, and all I could hear was my mom singing:

> *See, when you forgive your imperfections*
> *And you've auctioned all your clothes*
> *And you look to see your true reflection*
> *You will be the one who loves you the most*
> *You will be the one who loves you the most, yeah*
> *You will be the one who loves you the most*

—Brett Dennen, "The One Who Loves You the Most"

DEAR READERS

I am so happy this book found its way into your life. In many ways this story is an extension of my own story and how I wish life could be and should be.

I did my best to handle each moment with loving-care. I did my best to make it clear that I'm in conversation with you. I did my best to make it understood that I'm joyfully witnessing you and honoring you for exactly who you are. I want it to be known that this book you are holding is anything you need or want it to be.

Where we meet is in-between the words. Where we meet is where you are.

The book you are holding is anything you need or want it to be.

medina

ACKNOWLEDGMENTS

Thanks to my teachers who saw that writing was my means for expression and encouraged me to follow my voice within. To teachers everywhere who make their students feel valued and seen. You make the world that much more of a beautiful place.

medina (they/them) is a Honduran born transracial adoptee. they identify as a non-binary asexual lesbian. they have a dual MFA in writing for children and young adults and non-fiction from The New School, and are a 2021 Lambda Literary Fellow. this is their first novel.

RESOURCES

Asexual Visibility and Education Network: AVEN hosts the world's largest online asexual community as well as a large archive of resources on asexuality.

GLAAD: GLAAD rewrites the script for LGBTQ acceptance.

GLSEN: As a student, you have the power to make change in many ways in your school and community. GLSEN works to ensure that LGBTQ students are able to learn and grow in a school environment free from bullying and harassment.

GSA Network: A GSA club is a student-run club in a high school or middle school that brings together LGBTQ+ and straight students to support each other.

It Gets Better: The It Gets Better Project reminds teenagers in the LGBT community that they are not alone and it will get better.

StopBullying.gov: Information for LGBT Youth: There are important and unique considerations for strategies to prevent and address bullying of LGBTQ youth.

The Trevor Project: The Trevor Project is a national organization providing crisis intervention and suicide prevention services to lesbian, gay, bisexual, transgender and questioning (LGBTQ) young people under the age of 25.

SOME NOTES ON
THIS BOOK'S PRODUCTION

The art for the jacket and case was created by Jake Alexander, who used pencil, paper, and Procreate for the Apple iPad. The text was set by Westchester Publishing Services in Sorts Mills Goudy Regular, a revival by Barry Schwartz of American designer Frederic Goudy's Goudy Oldstyle. The latter was released in 1915 and was an instantaneous success – noted especially for its suitability for newspaper advertising sections because of its efficient use of space. The display was set in Laterlocks Regular, a ligature serif designed by Hendry Juanda for Letterhend. The book was printed on FSC™-certified 98gsm Yunshidai Ivory woodfree paper and bound in China.

Production was supervised by
Leslie Cohen and Freesia Blizard
Book interiors designed by Christine Kettner
Edited by Nick Thomas

LEVINE QUERIDO